Blood, Sweat, and Steel

Tales of Future Combat and Mechanized Warfare

Three Ravens Publishing
Chickamauga GA USA

Table of Contents

Publishers Note

It isn't everyday that you get to work with one of literature's greatest writers, let alone one who literally defined the genre of Military Science Fiction with his Hammer's Slammers series.

I count myself lucky to have gotten the opportunity to correspond with David Drake prior to his passing, and to bring young writers his words of wisdom on writing stories in the genre.

His presence will be missed, but his legacy will live on through his works.

R.I.P. David

Dedicated to
David Drake

"Life's a forge, boy, and the purest metal comes from the hottest fire."
—David Drake, The Complete Hammer's Slammers Volume 1

Starting Out
By: David Drake

Some of you may want to become writers. I've known plenty of writers with that determination, starting when I was in high school. In my experience it doesn't help. Writing is hard work; it takes grinding away at it. The initial rewards are going to be pretty slight at the beginning, but this depends on what coin you want to be paid in. Money is a common choice but a desire for fame is probably even more common. If the latter is what you want, it isn't hard to find somebody to publish a story, probably online. Then you can tell people you're a writer. That's perfectly honest.

I wasn't into doing that when I was starting out, but I did give a story to Stu Schiff when he was getting Whispers going. I told him that unless he paid something he would get submissions only from people who didn't think they'd ever be good enough to be paid. He took my advice and I'm proud of that. And proud of what Whispers became at a penny a word.

People ask me about writing courses and writing groups. Some people swear by them. Maybe they're right but I never had courses on writing. I laughed at the girl who moved into the area and wanted to join a group of writers. Three of us locally did sell fiction and we sometimes got together socially--but the writing we did when we were alone.

In my experience, writing groups provide wannabes with a support group to tell them how good they are, and to make the leader or central figure (generally a writer who's had some commercial success) feel important. Do they help people write better? Not that I've seen. So how did I learn to write? I found good stories and broke them into their elements to retell them orally in eight minutes. I decided what was good by what struck me as good.

Military SF wasn't a category at the time, so I didn't try to write it, but there were a few really good examples of what became Military SF. And from one of these, Heinlein's Starship Soldiers (later Starship Troopers), I took the naming convention of the unit commander followed by an alliterative collective name for the unit.

I wrote Military SF because I'm a Vietnam vet. This wasn't common in the SF field in the '70s, but I'd been drafted into an elite unit and served with the best. A lot of people were hostile to 'Nam vets when we came back (it certainly wasn't a smart career move).

But 'Nam certainly gave me something to write about. If you don't write about what you care about, you won't keep up the grinding work that a writing career demands. Karl Edward Wagner had early praise and success. He decided after a while that he wanted a higher class of fans than (the mostly adolescent males) he was getting as a heroic fantasy writer. He switched to horror and wrote it very well, but that's not where his heart was. Others decided that the money wasn't coming fast enough or big enough. It's really a lot of work if you're going to keep at it.

Unlike Karl, I got something out of writing that wasn't available to me anywhere else. I'd come back from 'Nam very angry. Writing gave me a socially acceptable way to deal with my anger. The anger wasn't going to go away unless I let it out. People who don't have something driving them are luckier but they're unlikely to achieve writing success after the first rush which Karl got.

I guess that's something I'd say to new writers: don't try to follow the latest trend. Write what you feel like writing. It probably won't sell. Mine sure didn't but in the long run you may create something worthwhile.

Dave Drake

And Those Like Us
By Kevin Ikenberry

Master Sergeant Ivan Petrovich's radio crackled to life, and his tank crew's boredom evaporated. "All Victory elements, this is Brass Hat. Recon reports first wave is crossing Phase Line Rommel now. Effective range for weapons in five minutes. This one's for Earth. Let's take it to the buzzards once and for all."

General Higashiyama, Petrovich thought with a grin. *Salty old bastard.*

His magtank and crew had dug into position on the far eastern edge of the Terran line. This position, heavily fortified by combat engineer detachments, was better than any he'd seen since the war began. Early intelligence had reported a massive column of insectoid infantry closing in on them, along with their rickety, nuclear powered cannon.

The buzzards finally came out to fight, Petrovich thought.

An eruption of friendly orbital artillery fire streaked down, snapping Petrovich back to the present. Thundering contrails, like thousands of screaming meteorites, plunged through the high, gray clouds and slammed into the advancing enemy. The field erupted in geysers of flora, fauna, and mud. Petrovich kept his eyes on the bombardment and pushed the intercom button with his lower lip. The screen around his face winked to life, showing the vital signs of his team and vehicle as green: ready for battle.

"All right. Eyes open, all frequencies ready. Vara, do not let that gun leave the kill zone. When the order comes to fire, hit any enemy target you can see. Crew report."

"Driver, ready." Collins, the new kid from Earth, called from the driver's compartment tucked inside the hull. He'd left Cambridge and a career in astrophysics to come to war.

<<Interface, ready.>> The female voice of the magtank's intelligence program spoke tonelessly. Some of the programs had personalities enabled, but not this one. Petrovich would not hear of it. One woman in the tank was bad enough.

"Comm and autoloader, ready." Cuarón spoke from her position to Petrovich's left, across the breech of the hulking main gun. A beautiful Mexican woman, she was completely out of place to Petrovich's eyes, but there were few better communicators. Her radios were set to combat specifications, and the magtank's electromagnetic rail gun was set to automatically pull ammunition from the bay at Petrovich's back.

"Gunner, ready. Sabot indexed, sabot loaded. Thermal targeting systems have the first vehicles now. Cannot identify them as hostile yet." Vara, the quiet man from New Delhi spoke into the microphone. "God be with us."

Petrovich smiled and switched his visorplate to the gunner's targeting system. In the green haze of the thermal image, vehicles were clearly moving. Thousands of them.

"Just like we do it in the sims, people." Petrovich grunted. "Good hunting."

The first volley of fire came from far down the Terran line to the west, as planned. The lead buzzard vehicles oriented on the fire and opened up their green plasma cannons. They were headed into the kill zone, and the jagged, rock faces of the mountains to the enemy's right flank would keep them from running. So far so good.

"I've got a strange target." Vara said.

Petrovich switched to the gunner's camera sight. "That's a tank, no? Interface, identify that vehicle."

<<I'm sorry, commander. I cannot determine anything beyond appearance at this range. The vehicle appears half-spheroid with one visible gun tube. There is no repulsor signature. There are approximately seven thousand of these types of target vehicles within the enemy formation.>>

"Looks like a tank to me." Petrovich stared at the image from the gun camera. *What in the hell is going on?* He angrily flipped to the command net radio frequency and toggled his microphone.

"Liberty Six, this is Liberty Seven. Confirm what appears to be a tank, repeat a tank, at azimuth of three five seven point two from my position, over?"

The reply from his battalion commander was immediate. "Roger, out."

There was nothing else.

Petrovich thought about pressing the issue but resisted temptation. He knew that the Interface was relaying specific intelligence reports in response to its programming. Battalion, and everyone else, was also wondering what his report meant. A simple tank should be no match for a hundred-ton Chevalier magtank, but appearance meant nothing. Capability mattered.

He tapped the gunner's shoulder. "Range that tank, Vara. If nobody shoots it first, that's your first target. I want to see what's inside."

"Identified." Vara reported. The targeting reticle locked onto and tracked the moving vehicle.

<<Up.>> The interface acknowledged that the railgun was properly loaded, armed, and ready to fire.

More cannon fire came from outside, and Petrovich stood in the cupola to watch the Terran line engage the buzzard attack.

"On my command, engage and destroy all targets in sector. Vara, the gun is yours." Inside his helmet, the estimated distance to the lead vehicles clicked down until the "in-range" indicator came to life. "Fire!"

"On the waaaaaayyyy!" Vara engaged the cannon, and the first round left the tube with a *whump* that vibrated the entire vehicle. Petrovich watched the tracer, burning brightly on the tail end of the round, as it flew straight and true toward the buzzard tank. The alien infantry scattered and flung themselves to the mud around the tank as it exploded. The explosion left a thirty-meter circle of fire around the vehicle's remains.

He keyed the radio. "Liberty Six, priority target all enemy tanks!"

Petrovich did not wait for a response. He settled into his seat and engaged the magtank's command and control system. Immediately, the graphical projection of the buzzard advance appeared on his screen. Petrovich felt his pulse quicken. The valley floor crawled with buzzard vehicles and infantry all heading for the line's eastern flank. Toward him.

"Holy shit," he said, glad that only he could hear himself before flipping to the intercom. "We've got their main advance coming right at us, people!"

His battalion commander chimed in. "Seven, Six, curl your line back on the hilltop. Prepare to defend the flank."

No shit, Petrovich thought. "We're already doing it, Six. Get us air support or we're fucked."

For a moment, Petrovich lost himself in the fight. *Identify, target, fire. Identify, target, fire.* As the enemy closed on his position, he engaged all of the weapons systems he could, even the smoke grenade system that never seemed to work as advertised. Vara said he was thirty percent spent on ammunition, and the gun tube was overheating. Petrovich ignored it and stood in the cupola, feeling his knees quiver as he watched the crawling mass of the enemy formation skirt the engineers' many brilliant obstacles and charge straight up the hill without firing a shot.

The buzzards are saving their ammunition for a close-in fight, and there's no place for us to go.

WHANG!!

The vehicle rocked from side-to-side, and Petrovich fell instinctively into the turret. "What the fuck was that?"

<<High velocity impact on the right forward skirt. Minimal damage.>>

Petrovich swung the XM2 .50 caliber machine gun toward the right so he could see from its viewport without slewing the main gun. To his far right, where no other vehicle stood in defense, was a whole goddamned division of enemy tanks. "On the flank!"

Cuarón was already on the radio, rattling off requests in what sounded like five different languages at once. Vara slewed the main gun to the flank and started firing a round almost every heartbeat. Petrovich listened to them on the intercom and buzzed Collins in the hull.

"You okay, kid?"

"Roger. My ears are quite killing me, though."

"Be ready to move when I say."

Petrovich saw the battalion shifting now, moving to engage more of the threat. Artillery streaked down into the fray, but the enemy kept coming in their black crawling vehicles and spheroid tanks. Enemy gunfire tore up the ground around the tank, more missing than actually hitting their target. Debris fell in great clods across the top of the tank, so much that Petrovich worried about the cameras and weapons on the turret.

WHANG!!

<<Right center impact. No damage.>>

WHANG!!

<<Right front impact, skirt two. Hull penetration.>>

Petrovich blinked. "What?"

<<Hull penetration. Repulsors operating at seventy percent and failing. Private Collins is dead, and primary hull steering is compromised.>>

The magtank listed to the right, but Vara continued to fire. Cuarón screamed into the radios. He nudged Vara's back with a knee. "Slew to the right! They're killing us!"

WHANG! WHANG!!

<<Multiple impacts, right-front turret. No penetration.>>

The damage reports loaded to his helmet visor, and Petrovich screamed. "I can see that! No more goddamned reports!"

A new set of caution and warning lights chimed off, and red light bathed the interior of the vehicle. With the repulsors at forty-five percent and failing, and the gun tube overheating, Petrovich knew it was over.

"Gun's down!" Vara called. "Switching to coax!"

The four machine guns mounted coaxially alongside the main gun began to fire. Petrovich took control of the turret. "I have them, you get the gun working!"

Smoke and debris shrouded much of the field, but he walked rounds into every black shape that moved. Three hundred meters away, four tanks emerged from the smoke with their gun tubes pointed at him. The machine guns had no apparent effect. All four tanks fired simultaneously, and the right repulsor failed, pitching the front end of the tank into the dirt with a thud. The gun cameras failed, and Petrovich stood in the cupola. The tanks slowed and refined their aim.

WHAM!!

"Gun's up!" Vara called.

Not dead yet, he thought and grasped the commander's override. He fired three rounds as quickly as he could, and two of the enemy tanks exploded.

<<Hull penetration. Hull penetration. Class Three breach forward right. Auxiliary fuel compromised.>>

The report snapped his concentration and he dropped into the tank. *Do not die in place!*

<<Repulsor power at thirty percent and falling. Two hundred seconds until combat ineffectiveness.>>

Petrovich looked across the main gun to Cuarón. Her eyes were wide and scared. "Get me air support, Cuarón! Now!"

She turned to the communications equipment, her fingers flying across the controls.

WHUMP!

A massive explosion from outside the hull sucked the air from the compartment.

"What the hell was that?" Petrovich looked up into the cupola's viewports as the second of the approaching tanks detonated in a shower of debris. Four more appeared through the smoke and haze of the battlefield, their guns aimed to Petrovich's right and firing round after round at something he could not see. Two of the enemy tanks exploded a heartbeat later. He swung the viewport to the right and actually gasped as the surrounding terrain erupted in a quick burst of artillery fire.

He felt the approach vibration of powerful engines through the hull of his tank. Without thinking, he swung the commander's hatch open and stood. A Legion cavalry command track swung into position ten meters away, its helmeted commander standing in the cupola and motioning for Petrovich to get down and button up his hatch. Petrovich hesitated as the cavalry commander held out a metal canteen and unscrewed the lid before emptying it over the side of their tank.

"No trooper ever gets to Hell, 'ere he's emptied his canteen." Petrovich smiled and dropped into his vehicle. The cavalry swung quickly into the fight, guns blazing. From their antennas, flying in the smoke and haze, a yellow flag with twin black lions rippled as the cavalry accelerated into the fire.

That guy gets a bottle, Petrovich thought with a grin.

<<Repulsors are minimally operational. Withdrawal to supplementary positions authorized from battalion commander.>>

Petrovich watched the cavalry disappear into the haze. "Interface, emergency action protocol. Disengage hull controls and back us out to supplementary position Tango."

WHANG! WHANG!!

Petrovich felt the seat give way and he crumpled to the floor. Pain seared through his right knee and the world threatened to swim away. Struggling to sit up, he said, "Report! Vara!"

Cuarón crawled over the main gun and pulled Petrovich upright, then removed his helmet. Something warm trickled down his cheek. "You're hit, Jefe. Vara and the Interface are getting us out of here. The cavalry is pursuing stragglers, but we've been given a cease fire order."

Petrovich shook his head. "Cease fire?"

"Command says the buzzards are fleeing the planet. We're going home, Sergeant!"

Petrovich said nothing, doubting their fate. As the younger woman hugged his neck, he found himself returning the embrace. At their rate of movement, they'd reach Tango in about an hour. Earth was a lifetime away.

Then the goddamned tank mired.

Two hours after retrieval, Petrovich dug out his last bottle of vodka and limped towards headquarters in search of the cavalry. Anybody that crazy was someone he had to meet.

On the long gentle slope of the hilltop assembly area, Petrovich leaned forward, staring into the black mud as he placed his hands on his knees and rested. A jagged piece of metal poked through his coveralls on the side of his thigh. Without releasing the neck of the vodka bottle in his left hand, Petrovich pulled the shard free and dropped it into the mud. Fresh blood pooled to the surface and trickled down his leg, mixing with that of his dead and injured crewmen. The wound was deep, but not painful. Medical attention could wait a few more minutes, Petrovich decided as the breeze freshened, and a low-hanging cloud pushed across the summit of the hill. As it passed, the first sight of Amaria's almost-blue sky in days winked through the clouds, and Petrovich saw the twin black lions.

Around him, heavy combat vehicles floated a few inches off the ground, their tonnage held aloft by repulsors. He snorted and licked his lips, tasting a curious mix of salt, blood, and cordite. A drink would have been welcome, but he did not raise the bottle in his hand. *Not yet.* The label was long gone, but the contents were pure and ready for a final celebration.

Goddamned cavalry, Petrovich thought with a chuckle. Limping into the ring of vehicles flying the twin black lions on their antennae, Petrovich found three young privates smoking cigarettes. "Where's your commanding officer?"

The men smiled. "Command track is on the top of the hill." They traded smiles, and Petrovich saw an American flag on their shoulders and paused.

"Your CO is there? You sure?"

"Positive," one of them said. "Front slope, smoking a stogie."

Petrovich tried not to snort and stepped through them. More soldiers gathered in the center of the coil, and a few shook his hand and clapped his back. Petrovich worked his way to the back of the center vehicle and could smell cigar smoke. Around the left side of the massive, two-and-a-half by six meter tank, Petrovich stopped at the left-front skirt and stared. Leaning against the front slope, next to the gun tube, a dark skinned woman with short black hair rested. She stared off in the direction of the enemy retreat. An American flag sewn onto the woman's sleeve caught his eye, along with a combat action badge and parachutist wings on her chest.

"Looking for your commander," Petrovich said.

The woman raised her hand, holding a cigar, and smiled, but said nothing.

Petrovich's temper flared as his injured legs began to tremble from exertion. "Stop fooling around and point out your commander, woman!"

She looked him up and down coolly, took a drag from the cigar and said, "You're kind of loud for a man who just had his nuts dragged out of the fire."

Petrovich was aware his mouth hung open for a moment. *A woman in command of American cavalry?* She glanced at the bottle in his hand and winked. "I won't tell your comrades a woman saved your ass as long as that bottle's for me."

Petrovich laughed at himself and his misconceptions. "I suppose so."

The woman nodded and dragged on the cigar, blowing smoke in his direction. "They had you hanging in the breeze out there, huh?"

Petrovich chuckled. "How can I argue that?" He saw the captain's bars on her uniform. "Ma'am?"

"I'm Vanessa Ransom." She smiled. "What's your name?"

"Ivan Petrovich."

"Russian? A woman in a tank has to be near blasphemy for you." She grinned.

Petrovich shrugged. "Permission to come aboard, ma'am?"

"Only if you bring that bottle and call me Vanessa."

Petrovich crawled up on the slope and sat next to Ransom. She was pretty and much younger than he first thought. On her boots were gold combat spurs. "True cavalry."

"Through and through," she chuckled and reached for the bottle. Ransom drank from the bottle, winced, and handed it back to Petrovich.

"Why the black lions?" Petrovich drank, and the vodka burned as advertised. "It made you easy to find."

Ransom nodded and reached for the bottle again. "Long story. Some Irish heritage, but not the kind we talk about at parties."

"Then I should have brought whiskey." Petrovich grunted.

"This is good enough." She took another drink. "Slainté."

"*Na zdorovie.*" He smiled. "Everyone seems to think we're going home."

Ransom took a long draw on the cigar. "What do you think, Ivan?"

He looked across the smoky battlefield. Out there among the smoke and cordite, down between the blood, the track grease, and the mud, was the blatantly obvious truth. There would always be another war, and good soldiers would be needed to fight it. As long as the buzzards were alive, the mission would continue. "We're not going home anytime soon."

Ransom grinned. "And those like us wouldn't have it any other way."

Contested Landing
By J. R. Handley & Liska McCabe

Second Lieutenant Jaxon Pierce, 3rd Platoon, Bravo Company
2nd Battalion, 506th Orbital Planetary Assault Regiment

I sat alone near my pod, clutching my traditional green notebook, a centuries-old staple for lieutenants. My ears rang as laughter and metallic clangs reverberated off the walls. The acoustics on these drop ships were shit. I watched the guys ready their gear; some sparred a bit to "warm up" for the mission. I should have been over there with them. I wanted to be, but in all honesty, I was nervous about this drop.

I looked over at Sergeant First Class Greer. Damn, he was one cool cat. He either had ice in his veins or the best poker face in the system. He was only a few years older than me, but while I'd been struggling through Aristotle and theoretical physics at the Space Force Academy, he'd been stacking bodies all over the galaxy. Our first meeting went about like I'd expected.

"I'll be blunt, sir," he'd said. "You made it through training without a recycle, so you must not be a complete sack of ass, but this isn't playtime anymore. You'll either make it, or you'll die, and if you get a bunch of us killed with stupid lieutenant tricks, I don't care who your daddy is: I'll kill you myself."

Most USSF lieutenants would have sputtered with indignant rage at such a threat from a subordinate. I found it strangely comforting. Not only did it speak to his dedication as an NCO, but it told me he would treat me as he would any other LT. That alone was refreshing.

I may have been new to the Orbital Planetary Assault Regiment, but the Reapers were in my blood. I could hide it for a while at school, but not in the Regiment. I wasn't just a legacy Reaper…I was *the* legacy. The name Pierce was practically synonymous with the OPA. Dating back to its inception, a Pierce had always worn the flying coffin insignia. I didn't need to look at it to picture the solo drop pod, fiery wings superimposed behind the teardrop-shaped capsule. I'd been doodling it since I was a toddler.

The pressure was intense. I couldn't look like some noob one-jump-chump. I would, of course, make mistakes, but I didn't have the gracious learning curve others did. When your dad is your battalion commander and your granddad was the regimental commander of the legendary 506th OPA Regiment, the expectations are much higher. When that's you, your troopers watch your every move.

Today was no different: the eyes of my platoon bore holes straight through me. They stared directly into my soul, watching me, waiting for me to fuck up. I had a lot to prove…or disprove. I couldn't let that get in the way of the mission. Clearing my throat, I addressed the fifty-four seasoned troopers from my platoon.

"Listen up," I shouted, louder than I'd intended, "you know the drill."

Shit, did my voice just crack? That's inspiring. Way to dispel that baby LT stereotype, Jax. I'm sure dad would be so proud right now.

"Right…" I said after pausing to take a calming breath. "The void freaks will be conducting a drive-by insertion, and Bravo drew the short straw. While they stir up a ruckus, we go in as covertly as possible. We hit the ground running and secure the landing zone for the main assault. We launch in five, so buddy check your gear one last time and get into your pods for a final pre-drop function check."

My troopers' response was suspiciously enthusiastic. I couldn't tell if they were mocking me or not, but as long as they followed my instructions, I didn't care. The platoon quickly set to work checking their weapons and armor before stepping into their drop capsules. Unlike theirs, my pod was reassuringly new. It hadn't been through the abuse of a contested landing on some backward planet waiting to flourish under the boot of democracy.

Running a gauntleted hand over my flying coffin's familiar black metal and ridges from the welded seams, I thought, *Maybe one day we'll figure out a way to make these things less deadly to the troopers inside.* I checked off the last part of my pre-drop checklist. I was about to step into the protected compartment when Greer tapped me on the shoulder. Raising an eyebrow at him, I waited for the grizzled veteran to speak.

"Sir, let me check your kit."

"I'm good, Sergeant Greer," I said, trying to sound more confident than I felt.

"Negative, you'll never buzz the tower with this soup sandwich."

Never what now? Where in the name of all that is holy does he come up with these asinine expressions? While I tried to decipher what he was trying to tell me, he tightened a few straps on my chest armor. He didn't say a word as he adjusted my ammo pouches, merely smirking as he caught issues I'd missed on my personal equipment.

"Now you look like a Reaper," he said as he smiled and slapped me hard on the helmet. It sounded like there was an unspoken "kiddo" in his tone, but I decided I didn't really want the answer to that question. His voice dropped to a conspiratorial whisper, and he leaned in close before continuing. "And don't worry, your dad was a soup sandwich as a boot LT too. Delta's First Sergeant knew him back then…you're in good company, sir."

"Thank you, Sergeant," I said with as much dignity as I could muster.

"Mount up, sir; we'll show them what death from the stars really looks like!"

Why didn't I think of that? Quoting the unofficial motto of the Reapers is a lot more motivating than what I tried with the platoon.

"Don't try so hard next time," he said as if he could read my mind.

I nodded in shock, turning towards my pod so I could lock up in my capsule. The delay in getting myself squared away showed; I'd barely had time to seal myself in when the countdown started. I quickly strapped myself into the seat, but it was sloppy work.

Gonna be a rough landing, I guess, I thought just as the drop light turned green.

Whoosh.

My stomach was in my throat in an instant. I'd simulated this exact moment hundreds of times in training, but the real thing was ten times worse. At least I didn't vomit into my helmet, so I had that going for me. I was just catching my breath when I remembered to check on the map overlay and adjust course, so I was over the target. That was the hard part, the part that the computers couldn't do for me. Well, they could, but I wasn't going to trust my life to some AI.

My pod continued to pick up speed as its own internal boosters engaged, adding momentum to the already dizzying speed of the initial launch. For the first time, I reconsidered my decision to join the "family business."

I could have gone to law school like Mom said, but did I listen? Of course not! I let Grandpa's war stories sucker me into a damn suicide pod!

"Gah!" I yelled at myself.

Get your fucking head in the game, Pierce! You're better than this!

Looking down, I realized that I hadn't linked my helmet to the pod. Reaching out an unsteady hand, I connected to the system and let the new data populate my helmet's heads-up display. I checked the readings again on the HUD and saw several lights casting a faint glow in my peripheral vision. *So far, so good.*

Thankfully, the system was about as simple as it gets. Green lights were good, red was bad; a handy feature when you're busy avoiding smacking into a planet like a bug on a windshield.

Just as I started to catch my breath, the threat warning system light in my HUD changed from green to blue. I panicked a moment until I remembered that only meant I'd reached an altitude where I could begin receiving real-time battlefield data. I panicked again when I realized that if I could see the ground, they could see me too.

It took seeing a steady blue glow in the corner of my HUD to comfort me. Small and simple, it read, "countermeasures: one hundred percent." If necessary, I could activate them by flicking my tongue against a lever in front of my face. I liked having that control, especially if it was the only control I had.

I put aside the sinking feeling of plummeting at Mach snot and focused on remembering how my new helmet was going to work. Any second now, the system would begin populating vital information: friendly IDs, topographical data, and potential threats. My world narrowed to that display, eyes achingly anticipating the first hints of intel from the world I was rapidly approaching.

My pod jerked violently sideways, hard enough to smack my helmet against the bulkhead, which resulted in my HUD blanking out for a second. I once again fought to stay calm as the adrenaline poured into my veins, and my stomach threatened to paint the inside of my helmet with that awful veggie omelet that I could inexplicably still taste. I wanted nothing more than to initiate the drop stabilization sequence, but I was still too high up. Just a few thousand more feet…

That thought really didn't make me feel any better. I was brought back to the here and now when my drop pod was violently buffeted by a small, sideways movement. My already iffy stomach threatened to mutiny as adrenaline coursed through me like a fiery river. I desperately wanted to thumb the button to stabilize the descent, but it wasn't time yet. If I tried slowing my drop pod too soon, I'd end up running out of fuel before the landing sequence. If that happened, I'd be riding a falling rock on its rendezvous with gravity. That was a path to an early grave, and I wasn't willing to meet my maker yet.

Boom!

Another jolt. Another smack to my helmet. This time it brought the display back online, and thankfully the information had fully populated. *Thank God for percussive maintenance.* I quickly checked my countermeasures—still full—and breathed a sigh of relief.

Just turbulence, not incoming. I repeated that like a sacred mantra. If those commie fucks were paying attention, they'd easily take us all out before we reached the ground. They may be a literal plague on the galaxy, but their technology made them a formidable opponent. Lucky for us, their reliance on tech made them less likely to do things like actually look at the sky.

I had to focus on the task at hand. Like all men about to go into combat, I psyched myself up with inane talk. *If we survive the insertion, we'll make 'em pay, and those commies will never shoot at my troopers again.*

"Kill a commie for my mommy," I muttered to myself.

Kaboom!

While I could never say it aloud in mixed company, I didn't actually hate the average citizen of the People's Republic of Proxima Centauri but dehumanizing them helped me prepare to do what had to be done. I couldn't think of them as real people, just "reds" or "commies," and because God loves a Reaper, PRPC troops wore red armor that made them easier to kill, with a conveniently placed aim point: the gear, hammer, and sickle that rested just over their hearts. It was the Almighty making them easier to kill. I knew that it was true because the media told me that was the situation. Journalistic ethics wouldn't let them lie; I'd learned that in school as well.

Kaboom!

I did, however, despise the People's Republic of Proxima Centauri. They produced nothing. They simply spread. They consumed, enslaved, and killed their way across every system they encountered. If riding this pod to my doom could help stop that, I'd happily make that sacrifice.

My breathing calmed, and eyes laser-focused on my display as a confident, eager grin spread across my face. Maybe I was a little late, but I was ready.

Another shudder rattled my head against the inside of my helmet, but my grimace of pain was hidden behind the midnight-black combat armor. The turbulence increased, and my stomach churned as my pod quickly approached terminal velocity. I thought I'd hit the gravity well of the planet, but my sensor told a different story.

Baboom!

Another airburst went off, causing my head to rattle against the inside of the cushioned capsule where I clung to dear life on my fiery descent into the insanity that was an orbital insertion to a planet's surface. I was riding a bullet that some fleet loser fired at the objective, praying that this wasn't the day I bit the dust.

My pod shook violently. Warning lights flashed; green lights turned to yellow. Countermeasures down to eighty-five percent. Definitely enemy fire. I knew that we probably hadn't reached the lower atmosphere of...whatever planet this was. It didn't matter. None of that mattered if I never made it to the surface. I took a steadying breath.

Small spaces weren't exactly my favorite thing, but I could deal. The cramped interior of the drop pod had very little room to maneuver, but the tight space protected occupants from a bad drop. My muscles were tense, but I fought back anxiety attack.

Trying to turn off my panicked inner monologue, I put all of my focus on the throttle controls at my fingertips and the readouts from my HUD. They were throwing a lot of lead our way. My sensors counted a dozen anti-drop-pod gun emplacements and more designed to shoot our ships. The fleet would have a tough go of it, but there was nothing I could do about it. That was a "them" problem.

You know what you need to do. You've been trained for this. I just had to focus on the landing so I could join my troopers and get to work.

Baboom!

I felt no embarrassment as I worked through a calming breathing ritual that would put a Lamaze class to shame. It worked, and I kept my composure as my pod picked up speed. I felt my heart pounding against my ribs as the force pushed me flatter against the capsule frame. My mind swam through thick, syrupy thoughts. *Should I brace myself? Should I try to go limp? Can I go limp?* The ground was closing fast. *Shit!* My pod was hit. I'd lost control, and I couldn't eject. Nothing was working. I considered firing the jump jets.

Think, Jaxon, think. What did they teach you in training? Right, initiate the emergency jump jet sequence to rapidly halt my descent and hope that the jolt activated the ejection seat. Maybe that would—

Then I hit the ground with a loud clang. My brain felt like mush, but I kept my eyes closed and studied my body for a moment before trying to move. There was pain, but not as much as I'd expected. There was something else, though…something more alarming.

It felt as though my body were swaying, bobbing, and somewhat weightless. *Am I dead? I hurt. Am I supposed to hurt after I die?* My mind rolled and swayed along with the apparent motion of my pod.

Then I understood. I was alive. But not for long if I didn't do something soon. I'd landed in the large lake near my landing zone. I was only a mile off target, but the water had saved my life—unless I sank to the bottom and couldn't escape this pod—but I pushed that thought from my mind.

As I struggled to unhook myself from my seat, I heard my troopers coming over the radio. Needing a better understanding of the situation, I focused on getting myself straight before worrying about my men. I brought up my HUD, which had been scrambled on impact, shutting down my displays and my ability to move. Several long seconds later, a self-test sequence started. Untold seconds after that, my HUD ignited in glorious light and began feeding data to my eyes. A moment after that, I realized I was no longer bobbing or swaying.

I hoped that I'd drifted to shore but doubted I was that lucky. I knew the odds were that I was sinking. Using my tongue, I toggled the switch to eject myself from my pod. It was a long shot that I wasn't expecting to work. My HUD informed me of the error: the landing hadn't freed whatever had prevented me from ejecting in midair. I was stuck in the damn thing.

"Oh, come on!" I roared into my helmet as I realized that my pod couldn't eject me. "Open up, you fucking death trap!"

I struggled, flexed, and shook myself like an angry alligator, but was still trapped in my safety harness. *I guess my harness job wasn't so shitty after all.*

Then an idea occurred to me, and I turned up the power output of my armor to its maximum setting and flexed my arms. I felt the pod give a little, but as soon as I relaxed, it settled back into place. A single drop of water landed on my visor. I watched it creep down across the vision of my left eye. It left tiny droplets in its trail that sparkled behind the dim backdrop of lights within my helmet.

For a moment, the world seemed to be at peace. The war raging on the surface didn't matter. My time was up. Everything was going to be fine. I didn't have a wife or children to leave behind. Dad would probably be more pissed that I'd fucked up my first hot drop than about my death. There were just too many deaths in the regiments for one lone lieutenant to stand out these days.

I thought about closing my eyes. I thought about relaxing. I wondered if I should let it go, quit fighting, quit struggling. It would be easy to drift off and let the water take me. Then my comm crackled, and my eyes shot open.

I strained to make out a few words breaking through the static. Something like, "Help!" and "…our flank!" It took a second to make any sense. Then I remembered why I continued to fight. My Reapers were staring down Death himself, and I needed to be out there with them.

I hadn't even been in the fight yet; I didn't deserve to go out all cozy in my pod. My comm continued to transmit static, and with it, my own shame and rage grew. No, I'll go out swinging next to my troopers.

With a roar, I flexed my back, my arms, and my legs in sequential order. The pod gave a bit as more water dripped onto my visor, but I was still trapped. *This isn't working…now what?*

If brute force wasn't working, I needed to think my way through it. I looked at my display again. All systems were functional except, of course, the ejection mechanism. *If it was jammed, the system would still be working, but this says it's offline.*

Drop pods were printed. They were launched like bombs. The troopers inside fell to the planet feet-first. The pods were tough enough to survive the heat of reentry. The enemy was shooting at us. I got hit. No, not hit, winged. By what? By a plasma…then it dawned on me. The hit must have blown the fuse. *I know what to do!*

All I had to do was get an electrical current to the charges, and I could blow the door off this thing. I thought back to my much-maligned electrical engineering class at the academy and got to work tearing panels away from the pod body. A manual would have been helpful, but I was pretty sure I could figure it out.

Sparks flew, and I winced as I twisted the stripped wires together, but it worked. The icon switched from a garish red to a comforting green. I braced myself again, knowing the blast could still kill me. *Time to go!*

I initiated the charge, and the explosion threw the door free. The moment I saw sunlight, I activated my jump boots and launched myself out. Going from bad to worse, I found myself surrounded by a dark, marshy liquid. I grimaced as the stench of decomposition assaulted my nostrils. It smelled…sticky. Incorporating olfactory senses into their suit was supposed to make us more situationally aware, but I'd have happily sacrificed that ability.

I tried to swim out of the swamp, but I was too heavy. I felt relieved when, a moment later, my feet hit the bottom. I checked my HUD, and it reported no damage to my armor. There were no leaks, much to my relief. I wouldn't drown, at least not today. Sighing in relief, I quickly secured my combat load and straightened up in the muddy water.

Not wanting to press my luck, I studied my display, which was still resolving the lake's bottom and the telemetry from my fellow troops. I'd only landed a hundred yards from the shore, so I began a slow, arduous march toward the enemy.

The trip wasn't without difficulties; my computer was having trouble catching up to the rest of 3rd Platoon, but I was able to receive enough of the details, and the battle scene became distressingly clear. The enemy had my unit on the run. The orbital defenses had killed a significant number of Bravo Company. We were outnumbered, outgunned, and possibly outclassed. But if we didn't accomplish our mission and silence those guns, the invasion was doomed…

The closer I got to the shore, the more data my HUD interface was able to discern from the surrounding area. For a moment, I wondered if I might've been better off at the bottom of the lake. The PRPC wasn't known for being kind to the Reapers they captured. Torture, slavery, mutilation, public execution—everything was on the table with the commies. Then I saw something interesting on my HUD.

Ahead was a line of retreating troopers, my brothers pinned down and digging in behind a small hill about a mile to my left. The PRPC soldiers amassed along an area only five hundred meters to my right. Reports from my company suggested that the commies were assembling something. It appeared to be a mortar, but it was huge.

"Shit," I murmured into my helmet, forgetting to check whether my comm was active.

I was tempted to give orders to retreat. The enemy could sit there all day long, lobbing explosives against my troopers until the hill was nothing more than a pitted wasteland. They had a reputation for expending ammunition like it grew on trees. Then I realized I hadn't transmitted anything since entering the atmosphere. I hadn't transmitted a single word. The commies had no idea I was here. They'd surely seen my pod crash into the water and were happy to let me drown in the muck. A plan began to form in my mind.

I turned to my right, parallel with the shoreline, and leaned forward. Speed was of the essence, but trudging through water was slow and arduous, even in powered battle armor. I checked my inventory and found all my weapons still operational. *Thank God for small favors.*

After I'd covered three hundred yards, at least according to my HUD, I took my bearings. While I took in my surroundings, I unlocked my rifle, attached the grenade launcher, and raised it to my shoulder. The PRPC had assembled their mortar and lobbed their first round from the infernal weapon. Reports filtered through my comms, allowing me a sigh of relief. The explosive landed behind their lines without hurting any Reapers.

Gritting my teeth, I pushed onward. I didn't have much time. The enemy mortarmen would be adjusting fire. They would walk the mortars onto their target if I didn't do something. Then the carnage would begin.

I slowly emerged from the lake to a horrific scene of fire, smoke, and destruction. The once-green landscape crackled with smoldering embers. My armor worked furiously to make sense of the surroundings, to peer through the ash and smoke, and to identify targets. A slight breeze cleared the air just enough to allow a target lock, and I squeezed the trigger.

DOOP!

The sound hung in the air for a few seconds, giving me time to dive for cover while I waited for the explosion.

KA-BOOM!

I could feel the heat and force reach my hidey-hole. The explosion was much larger than it should have been. I'd missed my target, but what the fuck *did* I hit? I poked my head up an inch at a time and saw the mortar standing proud and tall, as I'd expected, but couldn't contain a surprised laugh when I saw the ammunition crate seven yards away going off like fireworks.

I clearly needed more range time with Sergeant Greer, but if I was going to announce my presence, that brand of spicy popcorn wasn't a bad way to go. I had to finish it before they regrouped, though. Emboldened, I straightened, reloaded, and lobbed another.

DOOP!

This time I adjusted my aim and shortened the fuse on the grenades before I fired. I didn't have time to duck before I heard the explosive report from my round.

BOOM!

That tightly packed group of commies made a tempting target, one even I couldn't miss. I had given in to temptation and was satisfied with the results. Bodies rag-dolled a dozen feet in all directions, the munitions causing secondary explosions.

Panicked enemy fire lanced the air and peppered the ground around me. It was a spray and pray situation, but I rolled to the side anyway. I dumped the spent cartridge and loaded my last grenade.

DOOP! BOOM!

That final shot was my own panicked response. This time I lobbed it in the general direction of the incoming fire, hoping to force the enemy's heads down long enough for me to find better cover. I ran, trying to get further behind the PRPC troops. I had to split their attention. With my comms still out, I could only hope that my troopers would see what I was doing.

BOOM! BOOM!

Two more explosions to my left threw me to the ground, the rifle clattering away from my grip as I fell. *Shit, grenades? Against just me?*

I needed my rifle, and I needed to return fire. Like yesterday. I high crawled across three yards of open, blackened, and scorched ground. I lurched forward, rolled onto my back, and brought up my weapon.

BOOM!

More grenades exploded around me but farther away. I breathed a sigh of relief as I realized they either sucked that badly or they weren't actually targeting me, which honestly seemed more likely.

Two red-tinged figures flitted ethereally through the dust and smoke. My sensors could barely register them, but the commies were running; they were retreating! Right…toward…me…*Fuck!*

The first red-clad soldier was less than ten yards away when he fell to the most unfortunate Mozambique I'd ever fired: two shots to the groin, one to his crimson-armored chest. Right onto the gear, hammer, and sickle that they'd graciously put on their breast. The second enemy ignored me, attempting to leap over me. Instead, he stumbled when I shot him in the knee. Two more shots from advancing Reapers stopped him before he could rise again.

The silence ended, and my comm filled with static. It was a voice, but that was all that I could make out. A Reaper from 2nd Platoon stood over me, pointing to the sky. I didn't know what he meant, but I took the second to stand and check the functionality of my rifle. Luck was with me; the weapon worked.

The Reaper in front of me tapped his helmet again, then tapped mine. I finally understood what he was trying to tell me. I still only had static—otherwise, my comm was down. I shook my head and tapped my helmet, indicating that I couldn't communicate. The other Reaper slapped me hard on the back, nodded, and pointed at the retreating enemy.

Two Reapers ran past me, along with most of the survivors of Bravo Company. They chased after more enemy soldiers, firing as they moved in buddy rushes. It would be a bloodbath, and I welcomed the carnage. I wanted them to bleed for every single one of my troopers I'd lost, and I still hadn't taken a tally of the losses from my platoon.

Scanning my HUD, I found Sergeant Greer and pinged him as the rally point for 3rd Platoon. He was behind the crazy charge but forward of my position. I gripped my rifle tighter and jogged toward his position. It was reckless, I know, but there wasn't time to secure the area first. I needed to turn this landing around and secure it for the rest of the regiment.

Dread set in as I closed the distance to my platoon sergeant. I needed to get over there but was not looking forward to the back brief. The numbers formed up looked distressingly low. I estimated I'd lost a quarter of my Reapers.

I took barely a moment to process the information scrolling across my HUD feed, glad my helmet hid my pained expression. I swallowed my rage and tried speaking to get things moving, but I couldn't get through the comms static. Growling in frustration, I did a system check to troubleshoot the issue, but nothing worked.

I broke the seal and all but ripped the helmet off my head, immediately smacking the biggest goddamn mosquito I've ever seen into the back of Sergeant Greer's armor with an audible crack. He quickly turned and recoiled at the small monster. Bulbous and neon orange, it was truly a thing of nightmares. The seasoned NCO quickly stomped the stunned insect into the dirt and stared at my bare face before stalking over. *I guess that's one way to get his attention.*

I touched my ears before he reached me, so he'd focus on the external speakers. I could tell by his body language that he wanted to tear into me, but I had bigger problems. Another wave of Reapers was inbound, and if we didn't take out those guns, none of them were going to make it.

"Reorganize the Reapers," I commanded before he got a chance to speak, "we've got to get back into the fight. I saw some guns our survey missed on the way in. We're going to take those out and spread the destruction down the line."

"Understood, sir," he said without a trace of the anger I'd perceived from him. He was as ready to go as I was. "Sergeant Bell from 2nd Squad didn't make it, so the battle net wants to spread his Reapers out amongst the other two squads. I halted that until I received your update. I'd say we're as good as we can be. I've taken the liberty of getting the company comms guy over here to fix your helmet, and then we're off."

"Why didn't you ask Reilly? Why go all the way to company staff?"

His eyes softened as he bluntly stated, "He didn't make it."

That one hit me hard. As a boot lieutenant, I worked the closest with comms and the platoon sergeant. I knew about Reilly's wife; I'd seen the vids of his newborn baby, and I knew of his plans to open a coffee shop when he got out. He only had a year left.

"Sir… LT… you need to snap out of it. Grieve later; right now, get your head in the game. Comms fixed your helmet; he's trying to give it back. I need you to mark the platoon HUD and update it with the targets you found."

Taking a deep breath, I nodded and then donned my helmet. Once I was back on the comms system, I updated the local map. I tried to send that up the company chain, but the command network wasn't responding.

Pinging my platoon sergeant, I spoke to him via a private comm channel. "I can't get through to higher," I said quietly. I wasn't completely calm but being back with my men helped. "We're on our own down here. The other platoons have their objectives. We'll take the new guns I pinged on the HUD."

"Aye, sir. Lead the way."

"I need your opinion, Sergeant. Do we take them out en masse and knock them over like dominos? Or do we split the squads and take them out as quickly as possible?"

"We don't know enough about what is going on. Send up one of our stealth drones to scout those locations, and then we can plan. Barring a large concentration of forces, we split down into our three squads, then we each hit a gun. Reorganize whoever survives the assault and hit the last two. We don't have time for fancy, so we need to go for quick…. Sir."

"Hooah," I said, nodding along to his recommendations. "Let's do that."

"Hooah? What the fuck even is that? Leave the motto to me, LT," he laughed, shaking his head.

I surveyed my assembled Reapers, noticing where my stealth drone operator was setting up his gear. I walked over and gave him my code so the data would display on my HUD as well as his.

"Loop Greer in as well," I said as I clapped him on the shoulder.

We were fairly close, so it didn't take long for our drone to get over the orbital guns in question. Sadly, the Space Force's definition of stealthy was far more forgiving than mine. On the drone's final pass back toward its docking station, a distant crack sounded, and it fell in a smoking spiral to the ground. Any possible element of surprise was officially gone as well. They'd be waiting for us.

I took a steadying breath and turned to face my NCOs. "I've assigned mission markers for the five enemy orbital anti-aircraft guns. I'll go with 1st to the gun marked as Alpha. Greer, take 2nd Squad to Bravo. 3rd takes out Charlie. We link up over comms after those targets are out, then regroup for the final assault."

From there, each squad broke off to prep for their assault. I walked over to Staff Sergeant Daniels from 1st Squad and listened to his plan. I didn't weigh in, trusting his experience. While he was speaking, I studied the Reapers in his squad.

"LT?" Daniels asked.

"Excuse me?"

"Did you have anything to add?"

"I think you covered it, Sergeant. If something comes up, believe that I'll bust your balls," I said, joking to lighten the mood.

I gave a quick nod to the other squads and then assumed my standard place behind Daniels in the middle of the column. I was in a protected position, in the center of the deadliest formation of warriors the galaxy had ever seen. We moved out, swiftly covering the hilly terrain to close the distance with the enemy.

As we approached our target, we heard the thumping from the guns blanketing the sky with their plasma hell, keeping our reinforcements from our small beachhead. Interference from the high voltage electricity needed to fire those guns caused a faint feedback whine of static to join the already clogged airwaves.

With no choice but to attack through the guns, I followed Daniels's squad as we pushed on. *This is crazy, Jax,* I told myself. *Why are we walking toward the guns like it's a Sunday stroll?* I had to push down the inner voice telling me to run and hide, smothering my inner coward. Ignoring that horrible sinking feeling in my gut, I focused on my helmet speakers. I didn't hear anything horrible when I focused on it, just incredibly annoying.

We marched on. The hills became larger, the dirt softer and harder to march through. I gave the order to halt as we came to a large red dune. I could feel the percussion from the guns through my armored boots. We were very close.

As I gave the command, I contacted Sergeant Daniels over a private communication channel. "Hold what you've got, Sergeant. I'm going to take a little sneak and speak. You've got access to my sensors, so you'll see what I see."

"Sir, that isn't advisable," he said, trying to dissuade me.

"It's alright. I've got this. I'm the most expendable man here; it only makes sense that I go." I knew Daniels meant well; he was a stickler for doing things by the book. After screwing up that drop, though, I needed to do this. I couldn't ask these men to do anything I wouldn't do myself. I slung my rifle and took my first crawling step up the mound.

"Negative, sir," he said more forcefully, yanking me back into formation, "that's not how we do things. I'm not letting my butter bar get himself greased on his first mission, and if you take one more step up that dune before we know what's over there, your face is going to meet Mr. Buttstock here. Understood…sir?"

I could only nod sheepishly, glad that exchange was private.

Daniels directed our point man to grant the squad access to his sensors and sent him up the dune in my place. As he approached the top, I took in his magnified view. I saw a single guard standing outside an outpost nearly two hundred meters away. It connected to a trench that hooked backward, clearly connecting to the gun's defenses. Zooming in, I saw the guard yawn hard. He was alert, but barely. Their defensive posture was overly confident.

"Why aren't they worried about us being here?" I asked no one in particular. "They saw us land; we've even killed a couple of them. What do they know that we don't? They had to know we'd do an orbital scan, and they just shot down our drone. So, do they think we can't see them? Right…what would Dad do?"

"He'd shut the hell up and kill a commie for mommy, that's what," someone muttered into the squad channel.

Fuck, that was over the open comms. Way to rock out with your cock out.

Ignoring the chuckles, I studied the sentry. I knew that if we moved too soon, the sentry would catch us and sound the alarm. Or start shooting. The armor would theoretically stop bullets, but I wasn't eager to test that theory. Either reaction could mean the end of my mission and the death of too many Reapers.

I waited as the guard shifted his weight from foot to foot, staring near where Jones lay prone. He never made a sound, but I was afraid any little noise might be too much. Their armor had enhanced auditory processors, just like ours. While we waited, I ran through every scenario and how I'd respond. The buzz in my ears had grown louder, verging on painful, distracting me in the most annoying way, but ultimately Daniels and I agreed on a plan of attack. He didn't like it, but circumstances on the ground didn't leave him with much choice.

The guard glanced around once more in our general direction, gave a hand signal I didn't recognize to the others within the trench, then noticeably relaxed against the rough rock wall behind him. *Why a hand signal? Why not just talk to them?*

I couldn't bother with that, though. Now was our chance. I looked at Daniels, projecting more confidence than I felt, and pointed up to the dune's peak. "Let's move."

The men needed no further encouragement. They quickly reformed the column and proceeded up the soft, sandy hill, stopping just before the top to reacquire our point man. The electronic whine was even stronger up there, intensifying as we closed in on the gun site. Painful pressure built behind my eyes, and it felt like my brain was vibrating. I could barely hear Daniels's transmission over the interference, asking if I was okay. All the men looked a little wobbly.

Then the sentry's hand signal made sense. "It's not the generators causing this," I said, tapping my helmet by the ears. "They're masking their location and jamming radio comms. It's only going to get more disorienting as we get closer."

Daniels paused a moment, then asked something I never expected, "What's your call, sir?"

"We go old school. Cut all comms. Hand and arm signals until we shut that thing down."

"You got it," he said matter-of-factly.

I wondered briefly if that meant he'd already come to the same conclusion and was just throwing me a bone, but ultimately it didn't matter. We had to do something, and that was all I could think of.

Daniels gave me a thumbs up, and I flicked my tongue to cut my commlink. Instant relief flooded my skull, and I was glad they couldn't hear my overly dramatic sigh.

I gave the signal for everyone to get into position, and I felt my stomach tighten along with my grip on dad's old combat knife. "This thing has spilled more blood than a wolverine in a rabbit pen," he'd told me once. Surely, it could spill a bit more.

We watched the guard. His posture relaxed; his head lolled with each breath. No better time to move. I gave Daniels a thumbs up; he flipped me off. I took my chance, and low crawled over the ridge towards the red-armored sentry. I made it, crawling like my life depended on it.

It did.

All of our lives depended on us taking out these guns. Fate was on my side because the guard didn't see me when I snuck into his trench. I froze as he jerked and shifted his weight. He didn't see me when he set his rifle down and stretched.

He certainly didn't have time to notice when I jammed my blade through the weak neck joint, pushing it through to the hilt. He barely noticed when his bottom jaw jutted forward, and blood poured from his mouth. Brain stem shots were always instantly fatal. No time to do anything but die.

The squad closed the distance quickly, arriving as I held the guard's limp body. The reality that I'd just killed a man set in, and I began to hyperventilate. Daniels smacked my helmet hard and motioned for me to quietly lower the body.

At his direction, I dropped the dead soldier into the thirsty soil and verified there was room to send the teams into the trench. A quick check of his person found no useful intelligence. Crouching, I moved swiftly to the curve of the trench and saw a good hundred feet; it descended gently below the surface into a tunnel before it opened into a protected pseudo-anteroom prior to reaching the orbital guns.

With hands flying like an Italian family at Sunday dinner, I managed to tell Daniels to keep one fire team to draw their fire and attention. I'd take the rest as the flanking force.

He shook his head vehemently, then slowly but firmly gave me the signal for Battle Drill 4-Alpha. I wanted to disagree. I knew my plan was solid and I felt momentarily incensed at his lack of confidence.

Then I remembered who I was dealing with. Daniels would never compromise a mission just to stick it to the new LT. I wasn't sure why he disagreed with me, but I had to trust he had his reasons. Shitty NCOs didn't last in a Reaper Company. I nodded once and returned the sign for 4-Alpha.

He organized the teams into a modified trench wedge—or whatever it's called—moved Alpha team slowly toward the guards, and lobbed his opening salvo of stun grenades.

The high voltage pulses flashed purple and blue against the reinforced dirt walls. As soon as they dissipated, Bravo team leaped forward, knives drawn, rushing the disoriented Reds with lethal efficiency.

There were no battle cries, no audible grunts. Stealth was the name of the game. Their deaths were quick, cold, and calculated, just like the guard at the entrance. Within seconds, each one lay dead, a thick arc of dark blood painted on the walls above them.

We listened for any commotion from the chamber beyond. The orbital gun's rhythmic thumping was much louder now. I smiled as I realized it would cover us nicely. I posted up with Charlie team by the entrance to the gun pit, Alpha team falling in behind us.

This was it. Our one chance to spike those guns, and we needed to do it fast. No time for finesse…we had to hit it hard and dirty, like a hooker on payday…or so I've been told.

At my nod, Corporal Young, Charlie team leader, tossed in a few flash-bangs, and we moved out like a well-oiled machine. Charlie team broke left, Alpha went right. As we encountered an enemy, the first man in the stack would engage, neutralize the target, then fall in at our six. We could search them later.

We rounded the next corner into the belly of the beast, and the gleaming sun, shining through the open roof, blinded me before my helmet could auto-adjust. As my vision returned, I counted a dozen enemies in different stages of readiness. Some were focused on firing that infernal gun; most were raising their weapons to greet us. In an instant, it was pandemonium.

My Reapers wasted no time, unleashing a storm of fire and blood within the subterranean fortress. Ignoring them momentarily, I brought my rifle up and aimed at the soldiers manning the gun. There were three of them, one adjusting the controls that aimed and fired the weapon, while the other two loaded the heavy projectiles and charge packs.

Weird, I thought as I brought my rifle to bear. *They haven't plugged it into the grid so it can fire more rapidly. Plug it in and add an autoloader, and the gun would fire continuously.*

Bang. Bang.

I fired two armor-piercing rounds, center mass, at the soldier carrying the charge pack, dropping him to the ground. Before his buddy could react, I fired two more shots into the one moving the solid shot projectiles. He dropped as well, twitching out as his crimson armor solicitously collected his blood. While I killed the two loaders, one of my Reapers took out the gun captain, silencing the weapon.

We breed Reapers to be aggressive, emphasizing violence of action over indecisive caution. Today one of the fools in my platoon proved it, firing a grenade at the Reds moving to replace them. Firing without worrying that we were dangerously close. The explosion threw my fire team backward, hitting the pit wall just as Corporal Young turned the corner.

Flashes of light danced across my vision as I struggled to maintain my situational awareness. If I lost myself to the welcoming bliss of darkness, I could die. My men could die. I had to remain conscious for my Reapers. *Stay alert, stay alive.*

Groaning, I sat up with my rifle at the ready as I scanned for any surviving PRPC soldiers in the pit. One crimson-clad warrior was just rising to his feet, but he hadn't noticed me yet. He never would either, as I fired two rounds into his back. At the same time, Daniels let loose the rest of the squad in a mad rush across the open space between entrances, taking advantage of the situation. His team reached the next room, firing methodically until each enemy soldier fell.

Blissful darkness took me after that.

I don't know how long I was unconscious, but I woke up to my helmet being removed from my head and Sergeant Daniel's blurry face looking down at me. He forcefully patted my cheeks, eliciting a groan from me. It hurt; he'd gone past hitting me and straight into bitch slap territory. I moaned in pain, not very manly, but I couldn't stop it. They could make fun of me for it; I didn't care anymore.

I blinked away the fog from my brain, allowing the world to slowly come into focus. "You can stop hitting me now," I croaked out.

"Good morning, princess. That was one hell of a move, letting Dirty Sanchez fire at danger-close range. It worked. We took out the guns with minimal casualties," Daniels said.

"Casualties?" I asked.

"Yes, the fire team you were with took the brunt of the force. The grenade left us with four concussed Reapers. Unfortunately, Corporal Young took some stray shrapnel. It caught him in the abdomen. We've got him stabilized; he'll make it until a medevac can get him out."

Shit…did we kill them all?

"If it didn't kill us, maybe it didn't kill them," I said as I fought off a wave of pain and nausea. "We need to—"

"At ease, sir," Daniels said. "This isn't our first rodeo. We danced the old bucket double tap, feeding them freedom seeds until it was forever lights out for those fuckers."

"Good," I said, trying to keep the pain from my voice. "Give me a shot of wake-up juice. We've got another target, or those reinforcements will never get here."

Laughing, Daniels said, "What do you think woke you up? Give it a minute, and you'll be good to go."

"Understood," I coughed weakly, "help me sit up."

I could hear the deep thumping from the other orbital guns going off in the distance. Each one hurt, knowing it could represent the loss of another brother. Using Daniels' arm for balance, I stood and took in my surroundings. I may well have been standing in the inner circle of hell, the blood, dead bodies, and pieces thereof adding a layer of eeriness to the morbid scene.

I took in the sight of the destroyed orbital gun firing pit, noticing subtle differences between this portable gun and the others I'd studied in training. This one was nothing like what I'd seen before: the gun was more compact and appeared to be mobile in ways that the others were not. It explained the lack of connection to the power grid and how our surveillance missed it.

I was no expert on the life of the cannon cocker, but I knew enough to recognize what belonged on this enemy gun and what did not. In the far corner of the area where we stood, set apart from everything else, was a strange device. Walking closer to it on shaky legs, I noticed a strange hum. The noise emitting from the machine was oddly rhythmic, identical to the interference I'd heard in my helmet.

Though less powerful without the speakers, it was strong and high-pitched, still giving me a major headache. I gritted my teeth and inched forward. The closer I got to it, the more intense the feelings got. I felt it against my skin, forcing my hair to stand on end. Ignoring it, I pushed forward, ever closer. *This would be absolute agony over the comms.*

"Sir, it could be an explosive!" shouted one of my Reapers.

I ignored him like I ignored the pain in my head. Walking up to the device, I was able to see the standard symbols that decorated every other piece of PRPC hardware. The enemy had used a strange paint when they'd labeled it, one that caused a visual distortion when viewed from a distance. Right away, I recognized it as an intelligence countermeasure.

"Clever, very clever," I murmured to myself.

When I was standing right on top of the thing, I could see the lettering, but I couldn't read their language. No matter how much my instructors tried to beat it into me, I was a one-trick pony when it came to my language skills. I knew enough to place the power source for this device; those symbols were universal. Stepping back, I brought my rifle to bear and fired three quick bursts into the power coupling. Sparks flew, floating into the sky before fluttering harmlessly to the ground below.

Almost instantly, the humming stopped. My headache receded, and the hair on my arms returned to its normal state.

"Sir," Daniels shouted over his helmet's external speakers, interrupting my thoughts. "Sir, the radio's back online. Put your helmet on; you need to call this into headquarters."

I turned, stumbling back towards where I'd initially fallen. I didn't have to make the return trip, though. One of my Reapers was walking to me with my helmet. He approached me slowly, staring at the rifle still gripped in my hands. Suddenly, he was in front of me, placing my helmet onto my head and sealing it tightly. I stood there, swaying in place, as he gently took my rifle and put it on safe. He nodded his head at me in that exaggerated bob people did when their facial expressions were hidden.

I braced myself for the feedback as I flicked on my internal comms and sighed gratefully at the silence. "Any word from the other squads?" I asked, hoping they'd had the same success.

"Yes, sir, they just reported in. Both of the other guns are down; ten more Reapers out. Three wounded, seven KIA."

"Can they press to the next objective?"

"Negative," Daniels shook his head. "Ammo is too low, us included, and these are the little guns. Those big gun sites have a lot more troops."

Though I was still fuzzy, I pulled up the drone footage in my HUD and began to formulate the beginning of a plan.

I nodded and turned away from the others to find a divot in the wall to focus my limited attention. Comms were open, but there was no way to know how long that would last. I couldn't count on getting another chance to update higher, so this one had to be perfect. No distractions.

I breathed deeply and opened the channel straight to the Company Commander. "Badger Six, this is Badger Three-Six, over."

"Go ahead, Badger Three-Six, over," came the commander's terse reply.

"Badger Six, three of the five orbital guns have been destroyed. Third platoon is yellow on both personnel and ammunition. I'm transmitting a list of our wounded and KIA to the tactical operations center now."

"Good copy, Badger Three-Six. Can you clear the last two targets? Our scans can't pick up their location from here."

I looked at Daniels, who shook his head.

"Negative," I answered plainly. With our numbers, a ground assault would be suicide even by Reaper standards. "But we can paint it for you."

"We'll be ready. How long do you need?"

"Two hours. Watch for our signal." I was about to say *Out* when a new voice broke in.

"Badger Three-Six, Thunder Six."

Dad?

"Go ahead, Thunder Six."

"Have your platoon ready for EXFIL at the following coordinates in three hours. Alpha will take it from there."

Wow, he sounds nervous. Maybe he cares more than I gave him credit for. That thought warmed my heart a bit, and I smiled inside my bucket.

"WILCO, Thunder Six. Out."

I turned to Daniels and switched to the platoon net.

"Squad leaders, listen up," I said with more confidence than I'd felt yet, my fingers flitting across the keys on my armored wrist. "Each of you grab two beacons from your wounded. You should be receiving modification instructions any second. Once those are fixed, each of you send them with two Reapers to my location. Then get the rest of your people to the rally point. Any questions?"

"No, sir," said each squad leader in turn.

"Good. Move out."

An hour later, after a too-loud fight with my NCOs over who exactly would take the mission, I found myself with three of my men a mere hundred meters from one of the two remaining orbital guns.

"Fuck me, that thing is huge," I blurted out.

"Yeah, with a lot more guards than the first three," Corporal Anderson from 1ˢᵗ Squad said next to me. "You sure about this, sir? We're not getting closer than another fifty meters, if that."

"We'll have to give them some left-right limits." I pointed to Anderson and the man next to him. "You two take this to the left flank. We'll go right. Turn it on, and we get the hell out of here."

"Roger."

We moved slowly, buddy rushing when we could, low crawling when we had to, but we each made it as close as we dared to the gun site. I activated the beacon, letting it flash an infrared code that our sensors could detect through the PRPC electronic camouflage.

Time was running out. We only had a few minutes to get clear before Hell rained down. We moved as quickly and covertly as possible until we regrouped at the safest distance we could reasonably expect. At that point, we activated the jump-jets on our power armor and ran for the rally point just as the first bombs carpeted the landscape.

We reached the rest of the platoon, still at a mechanically enhanced sprint, just as they loaded the last Reapers aboard the EVAC bird. I forced myself to slow down, ensuring my men would make it on board before me.

I turned to take one final look at the path and saw giant clouds of black smoke billowing into the sky. That's when Greer grabbed my sling and yanked me off my feet into the craft.

"No time for sightseeing, sir." He said, before turning and yelling to the cockpit, "All clear!"

Seconds later, we were airborne, bound for our ship right as the next wave of Reapers approached the planet. I didn't know if it was stress or the concussion I'd been fighting off, but exhaustion overtook me.

As my eyes closed, Greer nudged me, his voice a conspiratorial whisper. "Not bad, LT. Good job."

I smiled my thanks and nodded off as we left the atmosphere.

A gentle sway slowly brought me to my senses from the most restful sleep I'd had in—well, longer than I could remember. I tried to stretch my arms over my head but found I couldn't move them. *The fuck?*

That certainly woke me up in a hurry. I wiggled my fingers and toes and craned my neck from side to side. Yep, everything still worked. Though the room was fairly dark, I caught a glimpse of myself in a mirror to my right and barked out a surprised laugh.

The swaying I'd felt was the fact that I had somehow been mummy-wrapped and hung upside down from the ceiling like a chrysalis. Obviously, my men had been busy overnight. I couldn't even be mad about it. Thanks to Dad's stories, I knew this meant they wanted me to "hang around." It was a touching gesture, in a way.

I pushed, pulled, and wriggled whatever I could move, which wasn't much, trying to find a weak spot but only succeeded in putting myself into a spin. I was still struggling when my door opened and bright light filled and burned my eyes, destroying my night vision. Grimacing, I was able to make out Greer's silhouette filling most of the narrow doorway.

He clicked on the harsh overhead lights and folded his arms. He said nothing for what felt like several minutes, though that was probably the blood rushing to my head. He just stood there, silently mocking me with that damn smirk on his face. Truth be told, that irritated me more than being strung up like a spider's meal.

I met his eyes when I rotated back toward him. "Something I can help you with, Sergeant Greer?" I asked as nonchalantly as I could.

"No, sir," he said. "Just came by to let you know formation is in fifteen minutes."

I had made another full revolution, still straining against my trappings. "I'm, uh, probably going to need you to cover that one for me."

"Not a problem, sir," he answered simply. He grabbed my sleeve to stop my spinning, then squatted down to look me in the eye. Holding up a small, two-pronged, silver bar, he said, "Next time you *do* come to formation, though, you should wear this instead of that stupid gold one."

The realization sank in as he placed the prongs to my chest and pounded it through my uniform, deep into the skin. My eyes crossed a bit from the pain, but I only allowed a surprised grunt. I barely noticed him placing a small folding knife in my hand before he grasped my elbows and spun me like a top.

I heard him laughing as he strode out the door. "Congratulations on the promotion, sir."

"Thank you, Sergeant," I weakly called after him. I somehow managed to open the tiny blade without dropping it and went to work on my bindings, all the while considering how I was going to get those assholes back for this. It couldn't be any of the lame, bush-league stuff lieutenants are known for. No, my revenge had to be good…legendary…old school.

I made a mental note to talk to Dad just as the cords gave way, and I dropped to the floor like a sack of potatoes. Lying sprawled on the floor, panting in relief, I yanked the bar from my chest and stared at my new rank. Maybe it was all the blood finally rushing from my head, but I couldn't help grinning like an idiot.

Damn, I love this job.

Suzie Lightning
By Morgan Chalfant

"I love you."

Private Elliot Stokes found himself frequently saying it aloud to the open air. He said it as if the person his words were meant for wasn't long gone. But she was. Suzanna Ashe had been dead for almost six months now.

Stokes dipped the ragged paintbrush into the dented can and continued touching up the decal he had adorned the giant leg of his lifeline with. That's what the hoplon was: a lifeline. He stood at the feet of the fifteen-foot tall mechanized war suit he had dubbed *Suzie Lightning* after the Warren Zevon song that thrummed from the speakers inside the cockpit above. It was Suzanna's song. *Their* song. A lot had changed in the world. Governments had collapsed, the human population was ravaged, Tzal became a world-killer pandemic, and Suzanna had passed, but "Suzie Lightning" was still their song. That would never change.

"Don't you get tired of that song?" Bill Grenville asked, gawking from behind him.

"Nope."

The thirty-two-year-old Army private shook his shaved head. "Only you'd find time to paint, Stokes. Didn't anyone ever feed you that old line, it's what's inside that counts? Hell, you remember that pristine Dodge Charger of Corporal Benson's. Looked like a million bucks but ran like a goddamn backfiring lawn mower."

"Just some touch-ups," Stokes replied, running a hand through his non-regulation hair. "She's gotta look beautiful for her last dance. Besides, she's got it where it counts. Deep down inside she's all Army Ranger."

Stokes brushed the finishing touches on the image. All things considered, the image of a black-haired bombshell riding a lightning bolt had turned out pretty damn good, especially when he'd created it over a span of four months with anything he could find. Scavenged paint from a ransacked Home Depot, a few loose brushes from an art supply store on Massachusetts Street in Lawrence, Kansas, and a couple stencils he hand-cut from pieces of cardboard—the one thing of which there seemed to be an infinite supply.

"Well, she's prettier than Big Cat's anyway," Bill shouted. "No wonder he's still alive. They can't tell the difference between that thing and the enemy!"

"Don't be bad-mouthing my baby!" Catlin "Big Cat" Sanderson yelled, patting the leg of his battle suit, *Cyclone*.

It was the heaviest and largest of the suits at eighteen feet tall. The entire outer shell was draped in viscera and entrails from the mutated Tzal it had slain. The legs were a tapestry of dried blood and other bodily fluids. Stokes didn't have the need to ask Catlin why he had chosen to decorate it like a Vietnam-era necklace of ears. Scare tactics, psychological warfare, cover and concealment among the throbbing enemy masses. Stokes didn't know, and he didn't care. He thanked his lucky stars that Big Cat was at his side.

In life before the collapse, the three of them hadn't been that close, but an apocalyptic event had a strange way of bringing survivors together. The Army privates had managed to appropriate their giant armored suits as they scrambled to escape the overrun Fort Riley outside of Manhattan, Kansas. While everyone else was commandeering jeeps, trucks, and choppers, they had ended up in a hangar on the far west side where the next-generation fighting machines had been stowed.

The Yulaeus Model-2100 Hoplon had only just been unveiled a year earlier by a multi-branch military-funded science team of technological savants lead by a Dr. Harold Yulaeus. The state-of-the-art, sixty-thousand-pound war machines were colloquially dubbed "Mobile Shields". The word was, four bases in the continental United States had been supplied prototypes for testing, Fort Riley being one of them. The other three locations were a mystery to the three privates. Stokes and the others had heard whispers early on when the hoplons had arrived—how many had been requisitioned, who was going to test them, whether they were going to be shipped to active war zones—but all had gone quiet with the grim onset of a new, unstoppable plague. And so, trial and error was the next step. They had learned how to operate the high-tech mobile suits on the run. Literally. But now they were done running.

Doctors called the global pandemic "Tzal". Everybody else just called it "The Shadow of Death." This colloquial name was popularized because of the strange, grayish-black rash that broke out on an infected person's skin. It was "like they were wearing their own shadow," Stokes had heard a news anchor say before civilization had collapsed. The whole ordeal was like something out of a bad science fiction movie—the fever dream of a mad scientist. But as everybody knew, but so few would ever admit, dreams could have sharp teeth. Shadows could kill.

Tzal was a microscopic monster. It didn't kill those it infected. That was the real problem. What it did do was cause massive mutation on a genetic scale. It affected everyone differently, but the results were always monstrous. Always deadly, whether through transmission of the plague or the slaying of the rare percentile of people who were immune. Immunity to Tzal was one thing, but no one was immune to death.

Stokes, Bill, and Catlin had no idea where the disease had begun. Did it escape from some government lab and go all Stephen King's *The Stand* on everybody? Was it the product of a meteor carrying some alien microorganism? Or was it simply Mother Earth getting tired of humanity's bullshit?

Tzal's real origins had been lost with the rest of the human race. And if the mutated, monstrous drones it left in its wake knew where it was birthed, they weren't speaking.

But they were alive. The hoplon project was a success, and Stokes, Bill, and Catlin all found themselves silently thanking, not God, who had chosen to sit out yet another cataclysm, but Dr. Harold Yulaeus and his team.

Stokes and Catlin ambled out in front of the demolished travel plaza they had chosen for their Alamo. Catlin's tall, lean frame was the opposite of Stokes's more compact build. The Red Ridge Travel Plaza was built between the main stretches of I-35 running north and south, and was constructed of heavy concrete, and brick. Most of the glass in the entire property had been broken, but the structure was solid, which in a world of shit, at least gave them a small paddle. The ceilings inside were twenty-five feet tall too, which seemed excessive, but enabled their hoplons to actually move inside, despite being forced to do some restructuring of the main entrance so they could enter. At least the building wasn't plywood and aluminum siding like many of the side-of-the-road shanty stores one saw while traveling vast stretches of the Midwest.

Behind Stokes and Catlin, Bill stood in the cockpit running a systems check on his hoplon, the *Vanish*. The advanced solar-driven power source continued to operate effectively. The war suit was sleek and light, colored a deep indigo blue with white accents. Grooves and runnels marred the armored carapace. Battle damage. A few buttons inside the open chest of the giant machine glowed in the rapidly bleeding darkness.

"How long before they catch up, you think?" Catlin asked, lifting his lanky arms to rub his tired eyes.

"Wish I knew. Probably not too long now. They're never too far behind."

"At least the sun's going down," he said. "We'll have the advantage."

"We could use it." Stokes chuckled. "Crash and burn, Big Cat."

"Crash and burn."

The two men bumped fists. He chugged half the contents of a scavenged bottle of Glen Creek Spring Water that was probably filled in somebody's bathtub somewhere. Batting Catlin on the shoulder, he handed the bottle to him.

"Thanks." He emptied the bottle and twisted the cap back on. "You know, I still can't help but wonder if they're out there." He paused. "Julie and Hadley."

Stokes dropped his head. He knew Catlin's story like he knew his own. The thirty-four-year-old man had lost his wife and six-year-old daughter. Unlike Stokes, however, Catlin didn't have the image of what mattered most to him sprawled out dead on the pavement. Stokes carried that image all to himself. They had rushed to Catlin's house, only to find a little blood and nothing else. With the horror of seeing Suzanna's body came some manner of peace, Stokes thought. A certainty that Catlin was denied. After months of struggling and fighting the Tzal, Stokes still wasn't sure who really had it worse.

"I don't know, Big Cat,"

"I keep seeing Hadley's face. I used to have this photo of her wearing my helmet. Damn she was cute. Then the image shifts in my brain and all I can see is that shit turning her into some demon."

Stokes sighed. "Yeah." He nodded. "I wake up screaming sometimes."

"I know. We've both heard you."

"Same dream," he responded. "Only one I ever have. For the last three months. Me and Su. The first night we spent alone was in the basement of her mom's house. Pitch black. Couldn't even see each other it was so dark. We lay there just laughing with each other. I think that was it. The greatest moment in my life. And then there's the…thing that lunges at her from the darkness and drags her away. I can't stop it. She's gone before I can even say goodbye."

"Fucking Tzal, man. That's what it does. It poisons the healthy. Destroys everything good about a person," Catlin said. "That's what I gotta keep reminding myself. What's coming for us…it ain't human…not anymore."

Stokes felt his friend's hand come to rest on his shoulder. Catlin handed him the empty bottle. Stokes snatched it and crushed it between his strong hands.

"Well, ol' *Suzie* doesn't take prisoners," Stokes said.

"Damn right."

The crushing of gravel beneath military-issued boots echoed behind them. They glanced back to see Bill approaching, his whiskey flask in his hand.

"*Vanish* checks out. Power's good. Solar batteries are still holding at seventy-one percent. A little grind in the left elbow joint, but other than that, she's good to go," Bill said. "You two good?"

They both nodded. "Yep, just rehashing old wounds."

Stokes tossed the mangled water bottle aside. Bill unscrewed the cap of the steel flask. "To old wounds."

He took a long pull from the flask and spaced out for a moment. Stokes knew the man had his own demons, without having to deal with the ones that plagued reality. The difference was they could run from the Tzal. Bill couldn't outrun the demons in his head. None of them could.

Stokes and Catlin had witnessed the bloodying of Bill's mental well in one flash of a Beretta 9mm pistol. Even John, Bill's older brother, had known it was too late to save him. Bill hadn't spoken a word about it since it happened. Apparently, it served him just fine to keep it buried—which in a normal setting may not have been healthy, but at least it kept his war face painted on.

"We could retreat again. See if we could find some more cover," Stokes said.

It was a valid consideration, even in his own condemnation of it. Still, he figured it was his friends' decision to make too. They had constantly made their choices together, and Stokes half-figured that had played another part in their survival.

Catlin shook his head and said, "I'm through running."

"Yeah, me too," Stokes agreed.

Bill was uncharacteristically silent. Bill fiddled with the pendant around his neck: a four-leaf clover dangling from a cheap faux-gold chain. Stokes didn't suppose he could call it a good luck charm, since it had belonged to Bill's brother.

"What's on your mind, Bill?" Stokes asked.

Finally, he reacted, his gaze rejoining the here and now. He cleared his throat and steadied his voice.

"Besides this place being a goddamn coffin factory," he said. "Barbara Crampton in *Robot Wars*." Bill stretched his arms to the sky and twisted his neck to one side, then the other. Popping sounds echoed.

"Jesus don't get him started," Catlin groaned.

"Now that'd be a way to go out," Bill chuckled. "Only guy ever to knock boots in a damn robot!"

Bill passed off the flask. Stokes accepted it and took a quick pull, grimacing as the burning passed over his tongue and down his throat. He practically threw it to Catlin. As Catlin sampled the liver eraser inside the small container, he coughed and passed it back.

"Christ, man," Catlin wheezed. "That's shit's deadly."

"Speaking of that, any major number of them get in here we're all gonna fuckin' die," Bill stated matter-of-factly. "Cheers." He upended the remainder of the alcohol into his mouth.

"I think we're gonna die anyway, buddy," Stokes said.

"Yeah…" Bill trailed off. "I know."

As Bill tucked the flask into the back pocket of his BDUs, suddenly, an intermittent female voice began wailing from Stokes's hoplon.

Proximity alert! Proximity alert! Proximity alert!

That voice may have been called Bitchin' Betty in operating systems from tanks to aircraft, but to Stokes, it was just Sultry *Suzie* looking out for their well-being. He sprinted to *Suzie Lightning,* climbing the dinged-up outer hull like he had done hundreds of times before. He dropped into the cockpit and hit a few switches on the side console to turn the audible alert off. He pulled on the control gloves, the inner scanner reading his biometrics, and looked at the radar.

"Shit, guys! *Suzie*'s picking up some massive readings on the radar. We're gonna have company!"

Bill and Catlin rushed to their hoplons. It gave Stokes a modicum of positivity to think that if they were the last survivors, at least they didn't know it. For all they knew, some gas station attendant was on the opposite side of the ravaged Earth staring up at the stars thinking the same damn thing.

Nobody would ever live long enough to get at the truth. The truth was, they were living on borrowed time, and that time had finally run out.

Stokes closed *Suzie*'s cockpit with the push of a button and slapped the communication earpiece on. Servos whined as the open sections of the armored chest closed and locked into place with a pressurized hiss. Beside him, Catlin and Bill positioned themselves and strapped in as well, the chests of their hoplons shutting for what they all knew was probably going to be the last time. These weren't just their saviors, but their coffins. They had known that when they had appropriated them—even if they never would have admitted it at the time.

"*Suzie*'s five-by-five," Stokes called out.

"Systems go on *Vanish*."

"*Cyclone*'s ready to throw some hate," Catlin said.

"I give it fifteen minutes until they come down here and wipe us out," Stokes said. "They're moving fast."

"Yeah, and once they do, we're gonna last another ten at best," Catlin replied.

"Well let's make 'em memorable then!" Bill's voice resounded over the cabin speakers. "Okay, quick weapon run down. Not much left, but I got a Banshee missile pod, my flamethrower, two .50 cals with about two-hundred rounds each, and my saw. Oh, and one Phalanx mine."

"That'll be good for kickoff." Stokes pointed. "They're gonna be on that ridge in about ten minutes give or take a few."

"I'll run up there and plant it," Bill said. "Hang tight."

"We're hanging."

The *Vanish* was the fastest of the three hoplons. Bill steered the war machine sideways, its gears whirring like an old hard drive, legs churning and feet digging into the asphalt of the freeway. He took off across the butchered terrain, each step cracking the pavement until he hit earth as he hopped a farmer's barbed wire fence. From the travel plaza to the crest of the nearest hill, the land was a corrupted epidermis, pockmarked with craters, spent ammunition casings, and splattered parts of the Tzal infected. The remnants of their multiple skirmishes with waves of the diseased.

"Alright guys, I've got a CS rocket, a claymore panel, a Hexen rocket pod, *Suzie*'s sural pack, and my Sixty-Mike-Mike, but only a few grenades left for it," he said. "Big Cat, what's your status?"

"Pretty rough. My .50 cals are about empty. The 75mm rotary cannon I've still got a chunk a' sabot rounds for. A couple of anti-personnel missiles. Assorted melee crap. And one big ass Bloom for the grand finale!" Catlin exclaimed. "Been saving it."

"I shored up the south entrance earlier with a bunch of concrete barricades, so this is the only way in," Stokes said, pointing to the mangled front doorway.

"Mine's planted," Bill's voice broke over the comms system. "Headed back now."

It wasn't a minute before the *Vanish* came striding into view and rejoined them.

"I took a peek over the hill," Bill said. "We've got lots of company coming."

Stokes nodded to himself inside the hoplon's cabin. The radar blip was like a massive green amoeba steadily creeping toward its prey. The moment was here at last. He exhaled sharply and switched off the safety protocols on the weapons systems one by one.

An eerie calm settled over Stokes. For a few minutes, the comms system went quiet. No voices. It was the silence of preparation. Each man must make his own peace.

Stokes turned his eyes to the photograph wedged between two control panels. Suzanna's gorgeous face. A red-lipped smile.

Wet hair. Head leaned in to rest on his. The red-orange carnelian pendant around her neck seemed to gleam of its own accord, despite the glossy photo finish. Soon he would meet her again, in another place, where the limits of flesh no longer existed.

"See you soon, Su."

Stokes knew the reaper was stepping on their heels now—they all did—and it wouldn't do any good to try to run. They would stand and face it. Death couldn't be worse than the plague. Stokes couldn't think of *anything* worse than Tzal.

"Looky there," he said, pointing to the ridge. "Big Blue."

Catlin and Bill scanned the ridge with their targeting systems, zooming in on the lone behemoth. It was a familiar face in the Tzal-infected horde they had been ripping apart for the better part of the last week. In their past encounters, the massive monstrosity had been seen barking what they had thought were orders through a series of weird ululations, whines, and gurgling.

"Son-of-a-bitch had a growth spurt since we last saw him," Bill said.

"Yeah, Jesus, who's under all that? Rob Gronkowski?" Catlin wondered.

Big Blue. The fourteen-foot giant was a mass of infected bluish-purple flesh with sallow yellow pustules spreading about its acromegalic extremities like a child had stuck gumdrops to the writhing limbs. From its heavy body and malformed head sprouted dozens of jagged bone protrusions, some as big around as softballs and extending outward up to three feet.

From behind him, more deformed heads began to rise over the horizon, bobbing on grotesque bodies, many of which barely resembled human shapes anymore. Limbs were withered like dried out raisins, while others were engorged and hyper muscular. Heads lolled like sickly wind-blown balloons, while others rode on necks as big around as basketballs. Mouths gnashed and hung open, drizzling caustic fluid over an already dying landscape. Tzal was a Cronenbergian nightmare.

"I'll take the hundred on the left if you take the hundred on the right," Stokes said.

"Sounds good to me," Bill said.

"When I yell 'Alamo'," Stokes paused. "That's our cue to fall back into the building."

"Here they come!" Catlin shouted. "I'll take the middle!"

Stokes and *Suzie Lightning* veered to the left, preparing to let loose a maelstrom of fire and lead. Bill branched off in the *Vanish*, keeping an eye on the location where he had placed the Phalanx mine. With the *Cyclone* being the bruiser of the bunch, Catlin took it straight up the middle.

"They're gonna hit the Phalanx in a sec," Bill said. "Get ready!"

Stokes and Catlin locked in with their targeting computers as Bill focused his attention on detonating the remote mine. The scope on the *Vanish* was exceptional. The mine appeared on screen in crystal clear clarity partially hidden in the dead prairie grass.

The Tzal descended the ridge, some slowly shambling on twisted legs, others bounding forward at an inhuman pace. Bill waited for a larger cluster to enter the kill radius of the mine and punched a button on his control panel.

BOOM!

One massive explosion shattered the air. Fire. Concussion. Red mist. Fine dust particles and chunks of dirt rained down for a moment, settling amid the blanket of pink entrails and burnt flesh. Blackened and severed body parts riddled the ground. For a split second, smoke roiled and there was an eerie hush, and then the rest of the horde broke through on their relentless assault.

Stokes took aim with his wrist-mounted 60mm grenade cannon and fired a spread of high-explosive rounds across the battlefield. The grenades arced through the air and exploded on impact, destroying large chunks of the infected wave.

"Sixty Mike's empty!" Stokes confirmed.

Catlin fired up the *Cyclone*'s 75mm cannon, spraying a stream of high-heat Sabot rounds across the charging horde. Shrieks echoed from the dying creatures. Bodies disintegrated.

"Heads up, firing my pod!" Bill shouted.

Bill flipped a switch, and the shoulder-mounted rocket pod deployed, six rockets ready to put a serious hurt on their fast-approaching enemy. Bill knelt in the *Vanish* and locked in on six of the infected simultaneously, firing the rockets from the pod one by one in quick succession.

Sailing through the air, the Banshee anti-personnel rockets screamed as they met their targets. Each one threw shrapnel consisting of tiny steel flakes and ball bearings in a fifteen meter radius, shredding the oncoming threat. Arterial black sprayed and the concussive force was enough to knock many over.

"Nice shot, buddy!" Stokes exclaimed.

"Cannon's about out!" Catlin declared.

"Fall back to the shop," Stokes said. "I'm launching my CS rocket."

Stokes retreated toward the front of the travel plaza as Catlin unloaded with the last of his 75mm cannon. He heard the pounding *chug-chug-chug* of the *Vanish*'s .50 caliber heavy machine guns.

"On my way," Bill replied.

The front line of the scrambling Tzal were merely fifty yards away now. They left their dead and dying behind with no thought of aiding them. The Tzal infected showed no concern whatsoever for their attrition rate. They sallied forth savagely.

"We're clear!" Bill confirmed.

Stokes squared up *Suzie*'s hips and sighted the center of the mutated masses. He locked the coordinates and hit a button on his control glove. *Suzie* had some lightning left.

From a turret on the left hip, he fired a single, short conical pod. The recoil shook the hoplon. The pod blasted forward, flying in a straight line. The CS stood for Cable Shear. Stokes knew what the rockets could do in training, and this was going to be much worse.

The pod cleared a little distance between it and the approaching army and split into two parts. The halves parted with tiny engines of their own, between them was stretched a twenty-five foot long, high-tensile strength cable. The moment it snapped taut, the two halves started their second ignition sequence, blasting forward again simultaneously. They dragged the line between them. The moment the multi-filament cable struck living matter, it passed through with very little effort, clipping dozens upon dozens of the plague-stricken creatures off at the waist. Mass mutilation.

The Tzal's numbers had diminished, but they were still vastly outnumbered. Stokes watched as the unharmed Tzal navigated around their mangled brethren, some tripping over sliced up body parts.

"That made a dent!" Catlin said.

"Yeah, not enough of one though," Stokes replied. "Get ready for close quarters."

Catlin fired the last of his armament besides his Bloom: a fire-linked four shot of simultaneous, close-range guided missiles. The missiles struck, ripping large holes in the wall of enemies, delaying the onslaught for a few more seconds.

"Time to get our hands dirty!" Stokes said.

Stokes watched the *Vanish*'s arm ignite a flamethrower on its right wrist, while the other hand was replaced by a massive serrated circular saw. The *Cyclone*'s disproportionate fists were its melee weapon. They were built to crush. *Suzie* had her own hand-to-hand weapon.

Stokes flexed his fist and flipped a switch on the control glove. *Suzie*'s right hand flexed into a fist along with it, and a panel on the wrist slid open. From it dropped five flexible blades, each about six-feet long, ending in weighted, barbed tips—a sural.

The three hoplons stood shoulder to shoulder, their weapons primed just in time to meet the Tzal head-on.

Bill shouted, "Barbecue time!"

Stokes had just enough time to see a stream of flame spout from the *Vanish*'s flamethrower, engulfing a cluster of infected, before he had to focus on his own problems. He sidestepped two onrushing Tzal and whipped the sural around, the blades sang through the air in a horizontal stroke that sliced them into multiple pieces. Blood splattered *Suzie*'s carapace. Stokes whipped the sural around and around, slashing his attackers to ribbons.

He dropped another half-dozen with a single swipe. Another two leapt airborne. With his other hand outstretched he gave them the stiff arm from Hell and stomped them into the asphalt. To his left, the *Vanish*'s gigantic rotary saw wreaked havoc. Bill obliterated one of the monstrosities with long ropy growths extending from its shoulders, splitting him down the middle like a rotten hotdog.

"There's too many!" Bill shouted, cleaving two more with one upward swipe.

Stokes kicked another backward and backhanded two more. The pavement bled. Black, red, and yellow fluids drained from severed corpses, pooling in the low spots of the asphalt and draining into the cracks.

Suddenly, as Stokes reared back to whip the sural around, something struck the hoplon like a battering ram. Whatever it was crashed into him from the side, just out of view. He careened sideways and crashed into the road. Sparks flew from metal grating on the asphalt.

"I'm down!" Stokes yelled.

"I'm comin'!" Catlin shouted.

Stokes heard Catlin's voice, but wasn't sure what he said, as his brain shifted into survival mode.

Suzie's voice droned loudly inside the cockpit. *Severe damage to right forearm plating. Moderate damage. Right shoulder socket.*

He jammed the controls sideways. *Suzie* rolled onto her back. He raised the legs, but before he could push himself, Stokes saw what collided with him. Big Blue. He kicked his legs out, catching the massive brute in the knees. Big Blue's legs shot out from under it, and he crashed down onto *Suzie*, raining down blows on the armored carapace with its massive fists. One of the bone spurs punched through the hoplon's body just below where Stokes's legs rested. Another crunched against the hip joint. The plague-riddled goliath was bigger than *Suzie*, but she was more agile.

Stokes batted away several smaller infected, their jaws dragging on the ground. The sural was snagged on something. A fist glanced off the hoplon's head, scoring the metal. Stokes hit the release and the blades disconnected. He had his right hand back.

He flung his hand out, palming Big Blue's malformed head. With the other, he drove a fist into the ribcage and did some clawing of his own, tearing loose several ribs. The thing never stopped its assault, as more infected piled on. Just as Stokes thought the army of diseased creatures were going to pry open *Suzie* like a can of tuna, two colossal hands came together, crushing half a dozen infected and Big Blue with them.

"Gotcha…buddy!" Catlin said with a labored voice.

The *Cyclone* hoisted *Suzie* up and put her on her feet, even as more descended upon them. Stokes stabilized the hoplon as he uppercut another attacking enemy.

"Thanks," Stokes said.

"Any…time," Catlin replied.

"You okay?"

"Nope." There was a brief pause as the two of them backed up toward the entrance of the travel plaza.

"Bill! Get back here!" Stokes said. "Alamo!"

Stokes watched as the *Vanish* came bounding back toward them, shrugging off more incoming Tzal. The hoplon's buzzsaw was no longer spinning, clogged with meat and bone. Suddenly, another big hulking Tzal latched onto the *Vanish*'s saw arm with a set of overdeveloped drooling jaws and wrenched it free.

"Son-of-a-bitch!" Bill shouted, using his good arm to springboard himself off the ground and not end up on his stomach.

"One of those fuckers got lucky, guys," Catlin said. "I'm bleeding bad in here."

"How bad?" Stokes asked.

It was then he saw a massive bone spike buried in the chest of the *Cyclone*. It was a bit off center, but definitely in line with the cockpit canopy.

"Goddamnit," Stokes uttered, waving Bill forward.

The *Vanish* rejoined them as more Tzal continued to rush in. They backpedaled, swinging the massive arms and legs of their hoplons like enormous cudgels. Tzal bodies went flying, skidding across the pavement, some getting back up, others nothing more than piles of dead, contaminated flesh.

"You two get inside!" Catlin yelled, practically shoving Stokes backward through the shattered doorframe.

The *Vanish* veered inside as Catlin plugged the entrance with the *Cyclone*'s massive girth. The Cyclone's fists were wrecking balls, swinging back and forth, pummeling the Tzal and keeping them from breaching the entrance.

"What're you doing!?" Stokes asked.

"You two take cover. I'm firing the Bloom," Catlin gasped.

"No, Big Cat," Stokes shouted, seeing the *Cyclone*'s arms fall limp. "Hang on!"

"We'll get you outta there!" Bill screamed.

"Thanks…for being my friends," Catlin sputtered. "I'm gonna go see my daughter."

Coughing from the open communication line filled Stokes's cockpit. But only for a second. It was all drowned out by a cannon report as the massive mortar tube on the *Cyclone*'s back launched its ordnance into the air.

The large shell narrowly cleared the awning. It sailed upward, spreading into eight smaller shells like a deadly blossoming flower at its apex. The shells whistled, plummeting straight back down like meteors. Explosions devastated the area. The entire front of the travel plaza was ripped apart in concussive force and shrapnel. The *Cyclone* disappeared in fire. Stokes and Bill were thrown backward from the rippling blast waves, crashing through the far wall. Stokes could hear the concrete peppering their hoplons as they skidded to a halt outside.

The staccato detonations ended. Nothing moved. Static hissed in Stokes's earpiece. As Stokes shifted in his cockpit, he looked over and saw the *Vanish* still moving.

"Bill, you still kicking?" Stokes asked.

"Yeah, but I ain't dancing anytime soon."

"Man, I'm tired of this shit."

Stokes could hear the servos in *Suzie*'s legs whining and somewhere, in one of the hoplon's sockets, gears grinded against one another. He crawled over to a mound of concrete pylons and parked *Suzie* in a sitting position. Bill navigated the crippled *Vanish* up beside him and the machine collapsed with a loud crash.

"My targeting computer's toast," Bill said. "Can't see a thing. I'm popping my canopy."

Stokes witnessed the armored plates of the chest cavity part and the cockpit open up. He punched up *Suzie*'s onboard short-range sensors and scanned the area for threats.

Threat level: Green.

"Jesus, Cat got 'em all, I think," Stokes stated.

"For now," Bill replied.

"Yeah…for now. They'll be more coming."

Stokes nodded. "No doubt. There's *always* more."

With a practiced motion, he triggered the canopy release, and *Suzie*'s chest folded open. The hoplon's outstretched legs were a tapestry of deep runnels, dents, and punctures. One hand was mangled with the pinky and ring finger broken off. The joints sparked, trying to move in unison, as Stokes flexed his hand. Then, Stokes couldn't help but crack a tiny smile—a smile between just him and his robot. Except for some red stains, the emblem he had painted on the right leg was unmarred. The paint glinted in the light of the numerous fires burning around them.

He unstrapped himself from the hoplon as he saw Bill limp up beside *Suzie*'s tree trunk-sized leg. Dried blood was smeared along one side of his forehead, and his hair hung in sweat-damp strands, but he looked okay, all things considered.

"What's up? You good?"

"The only way I'll be good is if you have any of that engine degreaser left," Stokes said, climbing down the hoplon chassis to the ground.

"You're in luck," Bill said. "Been saving this. Special occasion, you know."

From the pocket of his army fatigues, he produced a small mini-bottle of Wild Turkey. Stokes smirked and shook his head.

"No time like the present, I suppose."

The two of them ambled around and relaxed up against *Suzie's* thigh. Stokes leaned back and exhaled. The adrenaline was wearing off, and his whole body was beginning to ache. Bill cracked the top of the bottle and put it to his nose.

"Woo! Will you smell that sweet bouquet!"

Stokes wiped sweat from his eyes. Bill took a quick swig and swished the whiskey around in his mouth as he passed off the tiny bottle. Stokes sipped the amber liquid, then tipped the last remnants out onto the shattered floor of what was once the Red River Travel Plaza.

"That's for the Big Cat," he said.

Bill nodded in agreement. There was a moment of silence between them. However unplanned it might have been, it seemed preordained the moment they set foot outside their hoplons. A moment of silence for a lost friend. For reflection.

Stokes saw Bill palming his brother's clover necklace, staring off into space like he was trying to figure out what he was going to say to John when they were reunited.

Moments later, Stokes found himself glancing back at the decal. Suzie was there, still riding her lightning bolt. Wild. Celestial. Electric. His mind drifted to the photograph he had forgotten up in the cockpit. *No matter*, he thought. *I have plenty of photographs of Suzanna in my head.* He could view them anytime he wanted. For so long, he had shut them out so he could survive—even though there were many occasions he didn't want to anymore. Now the surge broke the dam in his mind, and they came flooding in.

Images. Images washed over his brain like a sudden bucket of ice water to the face. Suzanna's smile underneath a sky of fireworks as they lay on a blanket holding hands. Their walks through the small downtown bookstore, sneaking kisses in the stacks and making fun of the awful titles of romance novels. Her perfume on nights of eating Chinese food and snuggling on the couch, each one another's world entire.

Stokes brushed away a brimming tear. He would see her again. In another life, in another place, where they were not hindered by the limitations of flesh.

Bill's hand fell on his shoulder, startling him. Stokes snapped back to reality. The flames threw shadows around the rubble, and he began to laugh. Shadow laughter. It wasn't the same without Suzanna, but it would do until she was able to laugh with him again.

Bill couldn't contain himself. He began to laugh too, even though he clearly didn't know why. Finally, regaining his composure, he asked, "Well, buddy, what do you want to do now?"

Stokes tossed the small mini-bottle out into the darkness—into the void where the distant sounds of the Tzal still carried. He rested his head back against *Suzie*'s leg and looked at Bill.

"Let's just sit here," he said. "And wait for the sun to come up."

Rules of Survival

By Casey Moores

Pop Up Threat

"BDA, we're fifteen out, prep for infil," Lieutenant Renee "Guts" Everett announced over the interphone.

"Copy, Jazz," replied her left gunner Jason "Big Dumb Animal" Colline.

"Hey, your options are 'Pilot', or 'Guts', understand?" she scolded. Normally, Renee was referred to by her crew position. Tradition allowed for the use of squadron-assigned callsigns. However, "Jazz" was not her assigned callsign. When BDA didn't respond, she could sense him smirking.

Pick your battles.

"Just get them ready," she said, gritting her teeth and breathing the anger out.

Most of her focus centered around maintaining position in the middle of the left side in a formation of six. Flying her aging MV-262 Destrier "Warhorse" at just over four hundred knots, in formation, a hair above the tree line, and in near total darkness using low-light vision would task most pilots. However, for the aircrews of the 67th Special Operations Squadron Night Owls, it was an average night.

Deep insertion of special operations teams was their standard mission set. So far on this mission, they'd covered five hundred and twenty-seven of six hundred and eighteen nautical miles. It was as deep as they could go without sacrificing capacity for internal fuel tanks.

All at once, Renee was wearied, bored, and wired. Seventy-nine minutes of flying low, fast, in formation, and on night vision goggles was exhausting, tedious, and uneventful. She'd intentionally kept the lead Destrier in the same position in her windscreen for the entire flight. For all she knew, Lead could have flown them all into Hades. It didn't matter, so long as she stayed in position.

On the other hand, she was wired with the knowledge that in a mere fifteen minutes the insertion would happen. The Destrier's would lower their ramps and the drop troopers would leap out. They'd soar to the target in wingsuits, and pop small chutes at the last second. Most of the landing force would be absorbed by their light exoskeletons, which allowed them to carry a much greater amount of gear than their airborne predecessors.

All she had to do was keep her eyes open and stay in position, but it was getting tough.

"Missile launch, eight o'clock!" BDA shouted on the encrypted formation interplane frequency. The previous eighty minutes had been silent. A weapons engagement was the only authorized break in radio silence.

"Confirmed, spitting Chuck Mike," called her navigator, Crewman Kazuo "Powder" Iwakuni. As the formation broke sharply away from the inbound missiles, a wide array of countermeasures popped from each aircraft.

"Three missiles inbound," Powder stated internally. "Guessing Plea One Fives."

"Origin?" Renee asked. As she asked, data came up on her feed from the Dash Five Destrier, the aircraft to her left. Three SU-41 "Fluxrunner" interceptors had, unfortunately, been just off their ingress route. The defensive systems, based on the tracking radar and flight profile, identified the missiles as PL-15 air-to-air missiles. The fighters launched a second round of PL-15's and broke off pursuit.

Lead rolled out and took the formation up into the sky briefly, dispensed more countermeasures, and reversed back down as low as they could go. An order came through the data feed to drop the external fuel tanks. Twelve empty drop tanks released from the formation and crashed into the trees below.

"Two missiles've bit off, one's still tracking!" Powder spoke louder and faster than usual.

"Missile in sight, it's tracking…Slag! Three's down!" the right gunner, Alexei "Roach" Ramirez called. The Dash Three Destrier, flown by Jason "FIG" Mirelle, had been hit. Its marker disappeared from her feed.

"Hit and crashed, or…" Renee queried.

"Just gone, Ma'am," Roach replied. "Fireball."

Renee winced but refocused on holding her position. "Powder, update on the second volley?"

"They've all lagged off, I think we've broken their tracking." Powder reported. It appeared they had escaped the line of sight of the laser and radar tracking network of the Central Asian People's Protectorate, or CAPP. "Confirmed, all PL-15's are down."

"Okay, crew, five out of six ain't bad, I think—"

A wall of tracers and missile launch plumes erupted in front of the formation. The fighters had driven them into it. Lead broke the formation hard to the right again, but that left Dash Four, Renee's aircraft, closest to the wall of curtain fire. She moved up and high on Lead's six in an attempt to stay clear, but it wasn't enough. A few shudders announced the left wing had taken fire. The plane vibrated slightly, and she heard the loud tell-tale rattle as her left gunner returned fire with his Dillon Aero .338 minigun.

"Left wing's hit," BDA confirmed. "Sparks from number one!"

"Exhaust temp on number one's redlining," Renee called to Powder.

No response.

"Powder!" she shouted. Craning her head back, she heard wind rushing into the cockpit. She barely made out the form of Powder, slumped forward in his restraints, motionless.

"Crew, check in with damage." Again, there was no response from Powder.

"Left Gunner's up. Left wing hit, number one's spitting fire." Instinctively, she pulled the emergency shutdown handle on the number one engine to ensure it didn't light off a fuel tank and incinerate the ship. She fought the Destrier's desire to yaw left and watched the airspeed begin to bleed off.

"How's one look?" she asked.

"Still burning."

"Copy, firing the bottle." With a twist of her hand, she dispensed the fire retarding agent into the engine. It'd be a mess for maintenance later, but it would keep them from burning up.

"Fire's out now," BDA said.

Content they were clear from the ground fire, Renee eased away from the formation and keyed a notification to Lead they'd fallen out.

"Copy," was Lead's single word reply via the datalink. The briefed minimum force required for the mission was three Destriers and two drop trooper squads. Since, despite the losses, they still had that, the strike force continued on.

"Right Gunner, you up?" Renee called out.

Again, there was no answer.

"BDA, check on Roach," She requested.

"Roger, I'm out of the seat," BDA called. "A few of our team members are pretty shot up. And, yeah, crap… Roach's gone. Just… gone. Looks like his harness got clipped."

"Copy," she replied with a sigh. "BDA, go strap back in. Powder's gone too, we took rounds through the flight deck."

Her navigation system blinked out and went dark. A diagnostic message informed her the navigation electronics had failed. Then, the targeting electronics failed, followed by another diagnostic message. She reviewed her systems' status and stiffened. With horror, she realized that the electronics buses were overloading and failing one at a time. Frantically, she began shutting down extraneous systems: life support, communications, and defensive systems. It wasn't enough.

For the entire mission, they'd been flying too low over the trees for the drop troopers to bail out unless she could bring it to a hover, which now she couldn't. Over open plains, they could count on their armor and exoskeletons to keep them alive when they hit the ground. However, in the trees, there were strong odds they'd get skewered on a branch before they hit the ground.

The only option left was a controlled crash. As she scanned about for a place to land, the computer that governed the number two engine shut off. As designed, the engine shut itself down. She clicked on the alarm bell, which should've always had battery power, but the bell didn't sound.

"Everyone, brace for impact!" The Destrier had gone deathly quiet, but she still had to scream the words to reach the back section. She prayed they'd heard her.

With no engines, there was no power for flight controls. In less than a second, the Destrier fell into the tree line, cracked violently through thick wood trunks, and snapped through thin wood branches. Strikes on the wings and sides made it lurch left and right turbulently.

Renee could've ejected as soon as the engine died, but she chose not to. It might've increased her own chances of survival, but then she would've been alone and miles away from any other survivors. She trusted that her aircraft's armor could stand up to the onslaught of timber. If she survived the crash, it was her duty to lead the survivors to safety.

A tree strike forced the nose down and flipped the aircraft over. The aircraft splintered through one last collection of trees before it slammed hard down on the ground.

Initial Actions

Renee's mouth was dry as a bone and overpowered by the taste of metal. For a long moment, she couldn't move or even open her eyes. Fortunately, nothing hurt—her body was simply numb all over. A bead of liquid ran sideways along her lips.

In her mind, she reconstructed the details of what had happened. Things came into focus, tunnel vision receded, and she identified dark lines in front of her. They were all perfectly perpendicular to the ground, as if they were trees that'd grown horizontally out of the ground. Oddly, the ground had a flat, vertical face reaching upwards, like a cliff face.

Idiot. You're sideways.

As if summoned by the thought itself, she suddenly felt the force of her restraints cutting into the right side of her waist and collarbone. The metallic taste and the drip running across her lips was blood falling to the ground.

All at once, her upper back muscles ached. A sharp pain pierced her lower back. Her skin burned where the restraints rubbed. Her hands were numb, and when she clenched her fist to see if she could use them, she couldn't. In an instant, they were engulfed in a million needle jabs. She fought through the pain and wiggled her fingers until she believed one had the strength to grip. She braced herself with her numb hand and used the other to release her restraining harness. The tips of her fingers still lacked strength, so she squeezed her palm around the release and twisted until it clicked. Her right arm wasn't enough to support her, and she collapsed to the side.

Sparing a moment, she reached back up and activated the embedded beacon. There was little hope any rescue missions would be sent for them, but at least command would know where they went down. This type of mission was generally classified "unrecoverable" if assets were lost.

After rolling onto her back, she kicked at the cracked composite glass of her windscreen. As she crawled out on her left hand and knees, she thanked the goddess for the gloves that protected her hands from the glass shards. It still hurt, but at least they didn't draw more blood.

Once clear of the downed Destrier, Renee rose up and assessed her injuries. Her shoulders ached but seemed fine. The sharp pain in her lower back seemed to be a pulled muscle and not an actual injury. She'd bitten her lip at some point, and it was slightly swollen, but survivable. The restraints had chafed her skin. That'd be a long term problem, but manageable in the near term. Satisfied she had no life-threatening medical condition, she went to check on everyone else.

"Hello?" she shouted as she made her way around. Someone banged loudly against the metal inside the ship. She could hear low conversation inside the cargo compartment as she neared the top of the ship. It ceased when she shouted again.

"Keep your voice down," came a loudly whispered reprimand from inside. She reached up, pulled, and then twisted the release handle on the overhead emergency escape hatch. Her right hand still didn't grip well. So, when she pulled the hatch free of the aircraft, she couldn't help but let the weight crash to the forest floor.

"I said keep it down!" Backlit by the soft green emergency lights, an angry face with short-cropped black hair appeared in the opening. She recognized him from the briefing as the squad's SMAW trooper. He adjusted the shoulder mounted rocket launcher slung over his shoulder.

"You're one to talk, banging away back here," she replied softly.

"Well, the damn ramp is jammed shut back here," the chisel-jawed, dirty-blond, dreamy blue-eyed sergeant said from further back. "And no one briefed us on this hatch. I guess we can go out this way."

She knew they'd received instruction on all the exits. They just hadn't paid attention. *No use pointing that out.*

"Wait here," she directed.

"Like hell," the SMAW trooper replied, and started to pull himself through the opening.

As the private struggled his way through the hatch, he cursed at the others to help push him out. She pushed through branches and worked her way around the tail to the ramp. Once there, she pulled four pin releases and pulled hard at the top of the ramp until it fell back toward her with a loud, reverberating thud. The surviving occupants turned to regard her with awe. She heard a loud bump from the outside of the escape hatch and noted the private's boots had snagged on the inside, which meant he'd gone headfirst into the ground outside. Maybe, at some point, they'd learn to listen to her, but it was unlikely.

The sergeant stood below BDA, who hung in his restraints with closed eyes.

"Is my gunner alive?" she asked. The sergeant recoiled when she asked and stood awkwardly for a moment before he looked up. He reached up, put two fingers to BDA's neck, and then nodded. The unconscious gunner shifted, and a knife dropped out of a pocket.

"Yeah," she chuckled half-heartedly, "my gunners always seem to have knives hidden everywhere."

As her eyes adjusted to the green light of the compartment, she found a dark shape slumped on the right wall, which had become the floor. It had the unmistakable dark coat and pointed cap of an officer. Two more dead troopers were slumped down across the right wall. She nudged Lieutenant Dzurissin, who didn't budge.

"Yeah," Sergeant Fellyn said in his deep voice and nodded grimly. "He didn't make it. Privates Li and Peters are gone as well."

He glanced at Private Wnetrzak, the rail gunner with the shaved head, who nodded as well and looked away quickly. She noted that the sergeant had Dzurissin's .40 cal M17 pistol on his belt.

The sergeant noticed her looking at it. "Yeah, I figure he's not gonna need it, and we probably will. Anyway, we need to pack up and get moving quick. For all we know, there's drones or troops on the way."

The lieutenant's corpse tumbled sideways, and his carbon fiber officer's sword slid an inch out of its sheath. Looking up, the sergeant smiled.

"You know how to use that?" he asked, grinning.

"Never used one this big, but I'll see what I can do." After detaching it from the lieutenant's belt, she looked back up at the sergeant. "Let's clear something up right now, Sergeant." He straightened as if expecting a lecture. "Obviously I'm the ranking officer, but I'm just a pilot. I'm a moron when it comes to squad tactics. As such, I'll defer to you in these matters. Is that acceptable?"

"Ma'am, I admire you for saying as much and appreciate your confidence," he nodded and kept his grin. "Mors Ab Tenebris."

"Mors Ab Tenebris," she repeated. Satisfied, she strapped the sword to her waist and walked up to check on her gunner.

"Can I get someone to catch him as I cut him down?" she asked. Sergeant Fellyn joined her immediately and put his arms up to brace the gunner.

"Now, ma'am, if he doesn't come to soon, he's just gonna slow us down," the sergeant stated. "Keebler, can you help me with this? Bubbles, you too. I have the sense the big guy's heavy."

Privates Holcombe, a big, bald man, and Bloss, wiry with short, curly hair, reluctantly trudged over and arranged themselves to support the large, muscular gunner. She produced a v-knife from her side and, when the three were ready, she cut the straps. BDA dropped into their exoskeleton-enhanced arms, and they set him gently to the ground.

"I understand," she said. "If you can help me get him a few hundred yards from here, I'll take care of him. I assume you have plans, with or without us?" The sergeant nodded.

"May I ask?" He stared intensely at her for a moment. "First of all, ma'am, can I ask if you can provide any insight into whether we can expect any rescue any time soon?"

"Not here," she responded, "They're not sending any rescue ships this deep until the CAPP air defenses are much more degraded."

"Well then," he continued sternly, "we're a few hundred klicks from the objective, so even if we could fight our way there, which is doubtful, we'd be about a week late to the fight. I think the best way is to evade CAPP territory and rejoin our lines. It's gonna be a hike, but it's the only way."

Before she could respond, BDA jerked violently and backhanded Holcombe's legs. The private fell backward and crashed against the upright floor. The others grinned.

"What the…where?" BDA searched around and keyed in on his pilot.

Renee knelt beside him. "We crashed. How you doin'?"

He closed his eyes in pain, grabbed at his head, and squeezed finger into his temples. "I must've had way too many shots last night. I didn't dance on any tables, did I? Wait"—his voice jumped several notches in volume—"I didn't pick up the tab again, did I?"

After shushing him, Renee smirked sympathetically. "No, your wages are intact, for whatever good that'll do you."

He blinked and rolled his eyes. Then, he looked around. "Dirty mother, did we crash?" She nodded solemnly as he looked down at where the right door used to be. "Oh yeah…Roach didn't make it, did he?" She shook her head. "Powder too, right?" She nodded. He pushed himself to his feet, breathed in deep, then slammed his hand into the belly of the ship with a shout. Then, he grimaced, tensed up all over, and rubbed his knuckles.

"Alright guys, this is great, but we gotta get moving," Fellyn shouldered a rifle and walked away.

"Wait, aren't you guys taking the big weapons?" she motioned around her. "We got the railgun, the SMAW, and the plane's got a SIG Sauer MG 338 machine gun in back that can use the minigun's ammunition. Plus…if I use the alternate protocol, I can put bullets through hard drives and light the fuel tanks to sanitize the ship, and we can hang onto the demolition charges we're supposed to use."

"Ma'am…demolition charges?" he asked with a raised eyebrow.

"Yeah. Before you ask, they're completely inert until we activate them, so stray rounds from below can't set them off. The engineers aren't *completely* stupid."

Fellyn put a hand up in frustration, "Okay, ma'am, either way, that'd all just weigh us down. We gotta stay light to get far away as fast as we can. We've wasted enough time already, we gotta get movin'."

"Well, yes," she conceded, "but we don't know what we might have to fight our way through. I say we at least get these weapons safely away and stash them somewhere else. If we leave them here, they're gone. Why not have them available if we need them?" She looked around at the group incredulously. "Aren't you guys in exoskeletons? Why's the weight a problem?"

The SMAW troop mumbled something to the sergeant she couldn't hear. Fellyn put up his hand and waved him away.

"I'm sorry, private," she barked, "do you have something to add?"

The private, whose nametag said "Szrebiec", shook his head. "No, ma'am."

"Ma'am, Private Szrebiec was, very improperly," he glared daggers at the private, "suggesting we leave you behind with the weapons." He raised his shoulders menacingly and jabbed a finger into Szrebiec's chest. "Private, when I want your opinion, I will give it to you, do you understand?"

"Yes, Sergeant!" the private responded. He seemed hurt and a little confused.

"Now," the blue-eyed sergeant said as he turned back to Renee, "Ma'am, I think you've got a decent idea. We have just enough of us to carry the weapons and a good deal of ammunition. Assuming, of course, that you can carry your share. Can I count on you to do that, ma'am?"

He flashed a rather charming smile. Had she been younger, she might have blushed.

"Of course, Sergeant," she helped BDA to his feet. "You gonna be all right, BDA? Think you can carry the SIG MG out of here?"

"Yeah, Jazz," he said with a heavy, pained sigh, "I got it."

"And stop calling me…never mind." She eased away from him and headed back into the ship.

The blue-eyed sergeant chuckled. "Ma'am, may I ask what this 'Jazz' business is about? Your nametag there says 'Guts'…which is it?"

"'Lieutenant Everett' works, Sergeant," she replied. "Let's leave it at that."

He put his hands up innocently. "Okay, ma'am, whatever you say."

Renee tried not to show it, but she loved the way he called her "ma'am". With a sigh, she went back to work in the aircraft. As the sergeant had said, they were on a timeline, and they'd already loitered far too long. As the others collected the weaponry, she pulled the sanitization charges out from their shells in strategically placed locations. A single bullet sanitized each piece of electronic hardware. She did one more headcount before returning to the cockpit.

She crawled back over the glass, knelt inside, and grabbed the Search And Rescue satellite radio, or SARSat. After it completed its initialization, she sent a databurst to ensure leadership would know their initial location and number of survivors.

"Ma'am?" Blue Eyes called out. "Are you about ready? We really gotta go!"

As if to underscore the statement, a small humming noise became audible and steadily increased.

"Drones! Scatter!" the sergeant shouted.

Letting the troopers deal with the threat, she verified the SARSat had completed the data burst. Flashes illuminated the trees and painted rapidly shifting shadows. The sizzling pulses of rifle fire picked up as she removed the last small demo charge and then blasted the flight deck's processor. The quiet, hollow thrum of a railgun was barely audible amidst the cacophony, but it nonetheless heralded an explosion and a rain of metal.

A piercing, ratcheting noise tore across the aircraft and she hesitated to crawl out. Dirt, with tiny bouts of flame, spat up from the ground out in front of her planned path. From her intel briefs, she decided it must be a CAPP recon drone.

When there was a brief break in fire, she snagged the demo canister and crawled as quickly as she could. After clearing the cockpit, she crouched and ran for the trees. She glanced around the edge of the tree and saw the large, pancake-shaped recon drone hovering, as if confused. A bullet would bounce off of it from one direction and it would swing to search for the shooter. Then, another would lance out from another direction, and it would swing around again. It stopped chasing the ineffective fire when it noticed her. Ducking back behind the tree, she heard a rapid staccato, felt the bullets thump against the trunk, and smelled charred wood. Finally, a rocket struck the drone from the side, and it exploded with a thunderous crack.

A third drone had sped in along the channel of destroyed trees, but when the second was destroyed, it promptly spun about and flew back off.

"Good job distracting it, ma'am," the sergeant stated as he ventured out from his hiding spot.

"I, uh…yeah, no problem," she responded, a bit dazed. Her heart raced—she'd never been shot at on the ground before. "Good shooting, guys, all around."

"Well, ma'am, you don't get to be a drop trooper if you can't make every shot count," Private Klein stated, with a hint of disdain.

The troopers magically appeared from the trees surrounding the wreckage and re-collected themselves.

"Sarge, do we really have to carry this stuff?" Private Bloss asked, somewhat meekly.

Sergeant Fellyn took a quick look at Renee and threw on his angry sergeant face. "Trooper, if anything we need this gear more now. Since they spotted us, they'll send everything they can to find us. We're gonna need some firepower to deal with those things. Now load up and get moving, people!"

Hands on his hips, he stood menacingly and watched his troopers rush about. Her gunner enlisted the help of two troopers, disconnected the ammo feed, and eased the boxes down. He then went to the back, where he unpinned the SIG MG, connected straps to it, and slung it over his shoulder.

"Ma'am, are you done doing whatever it was you were doing?" the sergeant softened his expression as he asked her.

"One more thing, Sergeant, I have to set the evasion symbol." She collected broken tree branches and laid them about the ground in a seemingly random pattern. "By the way, which way are you planning on taking us?"

He quickly wiped a condescending look off his face. "Uh, okay ma'am." He pointed. "That way. Denser vegetation…map makes it look like there's more streams to cross, better to hide our tracks."

"Okay, then." After looking in the direction he'd pointed, she looked back down to her artwork and rearranged a couple sticks. "All right, I'm ready, Sergeant Fellyn. Lead on."

Hounded

They made good time for the first few kilometers as the terrain was a gentle downhill slope through scattered trees and light bushes. As they neared the first stream, the undergrowth thickened. Three troopers who weren't carrying ammunition led the way and pushed through the bramble. There was some effort to leave as little trace as possible, but it was pretty futile and difficult in the darkness.

As the group spread out, the sergeant stayed near the front, navigating and directing. While they trudged along, staggered and silent as they could be, Renee pulled out her own compass and tied it to herself with some cord. No one else seemed to be backing up his navigation, so she decided to. The first time they made a major turn, she stopped to set up another symbol and made another report via the SARSat.

With little to do and the group eerily silent, her thoughts wandered. Light slowly grew in the forest. She watched the birds flutter through the trees, at first to verify they weren't enemy drones, but later just to watch them. It became a game to identify their colors, sizes, and the like. As she became familiar with the sounds of the birds, she focused on discerning the sounds of other animals. Small lizards constantly raced through the trees, occasionally leaping across branches. Somewhere, further out in the trees was something larger and faster, tapping through the undergrowth as it ran along, maybe a few hundred yards to their right. As she listened more intently, she realized she could actually hear several.

The trooper in front of her, nicknamed Crack, twisted his head sharply to the right and snapped his fingers. All the others stopped as well and spun to look at him. He pointed and they searched. The whine of numerous tiny motors echoed through the trees. A dozen yards away, a branch cracked, and a large set of black, metallic jaws jutted out from behind it.

"Night Hounds! Run!" Shouted Private Klein, the one they called Daddy's Boy.

One of their intel briefings had detailed the JS-23 Robot Sentry, nicknamed the "Night Hound" by alliance forces due to its black paint and four legged configuration. They usually carried a QBZ-95 assault rifle mounted on their back, but their fiercest feature were the vicious jaws that could tear through even the most advanced body armor.

"That way, up to that ridge!" directed Sergeant Fellyn. He led the way and charged up the relatively shallow slope toward a line of rocks. The railgun trooper behind her, Private Wnetrzak or "Trick", passed her up. A moment later, Private Opp passed her up as well. Simultaneously embarrassed that she couldn't keep up and fearing for her life, she drove herself harder. Her legs burned as she pumped them up the slope. She dared not look back but could hear the sound of snapping twigs growing loud and numerous.

A cacophony of machine gun fire opened up behind them. They tore into the private on her left, who spasmed and dropped. Reflexively, she flattened into the ground and heard the puffs of dirt as bullets walked up the hill beside her. When that abated, she sprang to her feet and continued up the hill.

From somewhere ahead, a rocket shot past, followed by a thunderous detonation behind her. This was followed by a secondary explosion and the clang of metal. Another fifteen feet up, in the line of rocks, the rocket launcher had been set up and Szrebiec worked to reload it. BDA and another trooper, Bubbles, snapped down the legs of the SIG MG and jammed it into a firing position.

"Jazz, down!" BDA shouted as Bubbles jammed in a magazine. BDA swung the machine gun directly toward her. She dropped. An ear-shattering ratcheting noise overtook all other sound, and her nose picked up a smoky, metallic smell. There were more *clangs*, but now the whines of motors were freakishly close. She rolled over and raised her pistol. As she had guessed, they were right on her.

From what she remembered in the intel briefings, the Night Hounds needed to be stationary for their targeting to be accurate. Their tactics usually centered on firing bursts to make targets stop for cover. Then, they'd surge forward to tear the targets up with those jaws.

She pointed the pistol at the closest machine, no more than a dozen yards away, and fired. Most bullets bounced harmlessly off to the side, but two cracked through the sensory faceplate with a loud sizzle. It twitched pitifully and collapsed onto its right side. Another rocket flew overhead and further back into the pack of Night Hounds. It exploded into a million fragments and sent metal flying all over. Flashes of rifle fire picked up as well, concentrated on the closest machines.

A hand reached out of nowhere, slapped down on her chest, and dragged her up the slope. Her legs scrambled underneath her in an attempt to half-crab walk backward up the hill. As she went, she fired into the approaching horde. One of her shots clipped a leg, which made the machine tumble on its side.

As the sergeant heaved her over the rocks, her pistol hand bounced on a stone, and she fumbled to keep hold of it. The loud *pop* of a shotgun deafened her. The sergeant drove the barrel into the open jaws of a metal beast that had reached the line and fired again.

Rolling over and resolving to be useful, she braced her arms on the rocks and aimed for the nearest hunk of dull black metal she could find. When Renee pulled the trigger, it clicked, and nothing happened. With embarrassment, she realized the slide was locked back, so she dumped the magazine and fumbled around in her vest in search of another one. While doing so, she saw the next trooper over dump his magazine, pull another from an open pouch on his chest, and reload in a quick fluid motion. He was most of the way through that magazine before she even located her own.

Continuing to dig with growing frustration, Renee took stock of their situation. BDA and Keebler were still ratcheting away with the machine gun, but the rest were all caught in melee now with the boxy, dull-black robots. Private Kraeckel, on the far left end of the line, had been torn open and two Hounds stood over him. They wrestled deeper into his entrails until he stopped struggling.

Finally finding a pistol magazine, she slapped it in and glanced to her right. Opp had driven his rifle into the jaws of one while Klein fired another rocket down the hill. Another Hound grabbed Opp by the torso, lifted him, and tossed him over the edge. He was ripped apart in the air before he even reached the ground. Sergeant Fellyn coolly dumped shotgun blasts into one robot dog after another. Wnetrzak stood between the sergeant and the SIG MG, and fired the railgun into the crowd that snapped away at Opp's remains. A line of the machines collapsed with holes burned clean through.

The area was a chaotic mess of acrid smoke, viscera, deafening machine gun fire, and screams. She grabbed a grenade from Keebler's belt and tossed it into the horde, which had thinned quite a bit. In fact, the Hounds in front of them were now down to a thin line. The problem was with the flankers. Renee was knocked forward by one, though it was immediately blasted apart by Fellyn's shotgun. She repaid the favor by sending a trio of bullets into a Night Hound that ran toward him from behind. It popped, sizzled, and froze.

The SIG MG ceased fire. The hum of the railgun quieted. Sporadic rifle fire continued for a few more moments and then ceased as well.

They'd survived. Though her eyes watered in the smoke, she peered through the dim morning light to see the last few Hounds as they ran off into the distance. She turned to check on the remaining troops. Her eyes fell upon the shredded remains of Private Opp: entrails, flesh, and bloodied armor were strewn about the space below the rocks.

Fellyn put a hand on her shoulder. "No judgment if you need to get sick. I'd like to say you get used to these sights, but you don't." He breathed harshly through his nose. "Mors Ab Tenebris."

"Are you kidding me, she—" BDA started with a smirk, but Renee cut him off with a dagger stare.

"Gunner Colline, what's our ammo status?"

BDA wiped the smile off his face as he looked at her. "Got plenty left, ma'am, but at least we got a lighter load now."

The sergeant nodded grimly in agreement. "Yeah, but less of us to carry it. We gotta move on out before they send more."

Evasion Movement

They picked up the pace to get away from the scene of carnage. The sergeant led them to one stream, and they tracked up the shallow water, balancing as best they could on stones to hide their trail. After tracking up a second, wider stream in a similar manner, they began to feel more confident they'd broken the trail. After a couple klicks farther across a ridge, they paused to catch their breath.

"Switch out socks again, troopers." Fellyn announced.

"This isn't gonna end, is it?" Keebler asked bitterly. "We're gonna die out here. If Night Hounds don't get us, maybe those damn drones will, or maybe even some proper soldiers. We'd've gotten further away if we hadn't been dragging all this crap."

"That's enough, Private Holcombe, knock it off," growled the sergeant. That the private had spoken up at all was a cause for concern.

"But he's right, Sarge," Klein continued, and glanced angrily at Renee.

"You too, Private Klein?" the sergeant said with an angry glare. Renee could tell the sergeant was trying to intimidate them into silence again, but it didn't work. His sigh told her he was going to try reason. "If it weren't for these weapons, trooper, those Hounds would've torn us to pieces."

This is going to turn bad quickly.

"He's right, Daddy's Boy," Wnetrzak jumped in, "my railgun here, that SIG MG there, they otherwise woulda chewed us up." Private Klein stood up and got in Private Wnetrzak's face. Holcombe stood up too, backing Klein up.

"Oh yeah, Tricky?" Klein practically spat in his face. "I bet the Hounds'd never've caught up if we could've dumped the dead weight and booked it. Opp and Kraeckel would still be alive if it weren't for that rich bitch over there."

Fellyn stopped, tensed up, and clenched his fists.

"Rich?" Renee chimed in. "Whatever gave you that impression?"

The group froze as confusion derailed the building rage.

"You're a goddamn pilot," he said, slower and calmer, "Who the hell pays for flight training who doesn't have rich parents? Or was it a sugar daddy?"

"Well, it wasn't one sugar daddy," she said candidly. "It was hundreds, maybe thousands for all I know." She took a moment to enjoy the look on his face. "I didn't screw them, if that's what you're assuming. Well, some, but that was always for the fun. I didn't take money for that."

Something misfired inside Private Klein's head. He looked as if he tried to form a thought and, possibly, speak.

"BDA," she said while glancing at her gunner, "why do you guys call me 'Jazz'?"

He smiled and actually blushed. Making a gunner blush was truly a feat. "Because that was your stage name, ma'am. Well, 'Jasmine' actually."

She raised her eyebrows. "There you go. My stage name. I used this beautiful body of mine to entrance you poor, helpless, salivating dogs out of their money. I grew up in the shittier slums outside LA. My parents, as much as they loved me, weren't getting me out of there. So I got myself out."

Klein's eyes narrowed. He had successfully formed a thought. "But I've known those girls, they pretty much—"

"Of course you have," she interjected. "Drugged out dolls, mostly. All by design. Most didn't even choose to be there, they generally showed up so high they could barely walk. It's how most of the industry works. But those like me are out there. We found we're better off acting like the others, so you never can tell…"

Her blue-eyed sergeant chose that moment to join in. "That's pretty remarkable, ma'am. It can't have been easy to get out of that place."

He's sweet. This relationship may need to turn unprofessional if we make it back.

"It definitely was not," she continued. "I came up with some rules. Or, rather, I collected some rules from some other girls, sometimes advice, sometimes, well…anyway…"

"Rule one: Stay away from the poison. No drugs, no alcohol—'cuz it's probably drugged—no mind enhancers or diet pills. To most bosses, it's a factory process. They get the girls hooked and get them to dance for drug money. Girl works for money, money buys smaller and smaller hits of whatever. Enslaved, easy peasy."

"Rule two: Hoard your money like your life depends on it, because it does if you want out. That actually worked in my favor. I starved myself to save money, which made me look strung out, just exactly what you sick whelps go for."

"Looks like you overcame that problem," Holcombe piped in.

She raised an eyebrow. "Are you calling me fat?"

"No, ma'am," Holcombe backtracked. "I mean, you're not sickly anymore is all, ya know, you're, uh…healthy."

"I'm pretty sure *healthy* is code for fat." She glared and feigned outrage.

"Easy, ma'am," Blue Eyes said. "I think what he's unsuccessfully tryin' to say is that you've filled out pretty nicely."

Big-eyed and innocent-looking, she said, "Oh, is that what he's saying? Do you agree?"

He grinned that big, charming grin. "I believe you were just getting to rule three?"

Renee smiled slyly and maintained eye contact with the sergeant. "Rule three: Choose your boss. Most are basically perverted slave owners. The real bad ones are *usually* easy to spot, but there's the occasional sweet talker who'll pull you in nice and gentle, then start slipping stuff into your food or drinks. Back to rule one. However, there are a few good, honest people out there just trying to make a living. Find them, make sure they know they don't own you, and stick with them if you can."

Lust obviously built up in those beautiful blue eyes, which was fine with her. Naturally, the others were all having their own dirty thoughts, but she ignored them. BDA knew better. This was old news to him, and she'd proven herself as the boss. At least *he* could be counted on. "So, I saved up and paid for some flight training, which got me into the Air National Guard. From there, I got approved to go active through one of those programs. Here I am."

"You're just full of surprises, ma'am," Fellyn said with a smirk.

"You have no idea, Sergeant." She winked.

They all gawked, lost and confounded. The argument had been completely forgotten, at least for now.

"Anyway, you guys all rested up, ready to keep moving? Socks changed out?" Without awaiting a response, she stood up and trekked off into the woods. BDA dutifully followed. The rest collected their jaws from the forest floor, glanced awkwardly at each other, and followed as well.

Men. I tell them my incredible success story of escaping hell with hard work and discipline, and all they see is a naked dancing girl. Ah well, at least I forestalled the rebellion.

Hidden Agenda

In theory, the "two-thirds" rule of moving along ridge lines was perfectly sound. An evading group moving along a ridge line was best served moving two-thirds of the way up. Moving in a valley would leave them trapped in a valley if discovered, and moving along the top made them the most visible. Two-thirds up the ridge would leave them clear enough of the top to avoid discovery. It also gave them a shorter distance to climb over the ridge and escape if discovered by troops in the valley. In practice, it was miserable. Ridges were not straight lines. Most were broken up by depressions, channels, deep ditches, and the occasional gorge. Great in theory, miserable in practice.

Every five to ten minutes, they were forced to scramble down a muddy, bramble-covered embankment only to scramble back up the other side. The long, evasive hike was exhausting. The ditches made it soul crushing.

After they dropped into one particular gulley—the seventh along that particular ridge—the sergeant led them along it rather than across it. Renee consulted her chart and realized what he was working to circumnavigate was a large, wide open space.

They stomped along moss-covered rocks and over a low berm. The sergeant threw a fist up and the contingent stopped. He knelt near the top of the berm, crouching and staring.

She took the opportunity to quietly turn her SARSat on and sent another databurst. Then, she crept up on hands and knees to join him.

Her breath caught in her throat. Out in front of them was a great, open field, just like the charts showed. It ended with another large forest that led up into another very steep ridge. Arrayed at the tree line were three SA-20F Gladiator surface-to-air missile sites, otherwise known as SAMs. Anything flying through this area, a rescue flight, for example, would be chewed up the way her flight had been. The ridge, almost more of a cliff face, was in the direction of the front lines between the CAPP and the Guard, meaning the SAMs would be perfectly terrain-masked from any inbound Warhorses. It was an even better setup than the one that had shot her down.

On the other hand, she could not see all that much infantry protection. The trio was set up as a Destrier trap, but the CAPP were confident that they were unthreatened by ground forces. A small, sneaky unit with a certain selection of weapons could, conceivably, take them out before they had any idea what hit them. The idea grew rapidly in her mind.

The sergeant turned to her and spoke softly, "Let's move away a little, I have an idea to discuss."

Her heart raced and she grinned devilishly. "All right."

He made a series of hand gestures to the team. She assumed it amounted to "stay here, we're going there." Seemingly satisfied, he motioned her down the hill and away from the team. The two marched a couple hundred yards and stopped behind a pair of trees where they could see the SAMs better. Renee had become positively giddy with the prospect of their small team taking down the trio.

"All right, Sergeant, s—" she started, but they spoke at the same time.

"I'm going to surrender us to the CAPP." Her world exploded. She stared dumbfounded at the gorgeous, blue-eyed traitor. "You said it yourself, they're not coming for us. The Chief tosses us into the grinder without a second thought. Dare to survive, like I have time and time again, and what do we get?

Sent out again for another chance at a meaningless death. If you're lucky, you get a shit retirement pay and a series of rejected disability claims for your broken body."

Her face relaxed and she breathed out slowly.

"The country you think you're fighting for is long gone!" He spat the words. "Just a corrupt system to keep the powerful in power and the rich, rich." The intensity in his eyes would have been intoxicating in other circumstances. "The Chief, the so-called government, the corporations, they all left you to find your own way out of hell." He pointed to the SAM site. "But the CAPP…do you have any idea what they'll pay for a defector?"

Her eyes narrowed briefly, but then she forced her innocent, doe-eyed expression back on. "You're saying this is our best way to survive?"

"Yes, that's right." He gripped her by the shoulders, held her tight, and stared fiercely into her eyes. "The CAPP has no quarrel with us, it's the Chief who has a quarrel with them. They just want to live peacefully out here, same as everyone else. With the help of the Chinese, their technology guarantees a good life away from the Chief's madness." He allowed himself a smirk. "And they don't throw people into meat grinders—that's why they use so many drones and the Night Hounds. Even those systems out there are mostly automated. They don't waste lives the way the Chief does."

Her eyes wandered in thought. She tugged nervously at her flight suit sleeves and then clenched her fists tight.

"Think about it, Renee. Right now, we can choose our own life. We can choose a better life, just like you did getting out of that hell hole you grew up in." He flashed the smile again. "I've seen you checking me out. We can be together with their protection. You and I can live in peace, raise a family…away from all *that*."

She couldn't maintain the facade, she was too out of practice. The anger in her eyes grew the more the traitor spoke. Boots crunched into the ground behind her. She half turned her head and barely registered Private "Daddy's Boy" Klein before she felt him grab her arms. He secured her arms behind her back with an iron grip on each wrist.

"I don't think she's buying it, Sarge," the snaggle-toothed private muttered.

"Yeah, I think you're right." Sergeant Fellyn sighed. "Pity, too. I would've really enjoyed putting babies up in there." He grabbed her neck with one hand and grabbed the pistol from her belt with the other. "I mean, I knew the lieutenant would never have gone along, which is why I had to plug him while we were crashing. Peters and Li were Chief lovers too. But I thought you…I guess I hoped…that you'd be smarter than that. Too bad."

A twig snapped further up the hill. Private Bloss innocently trekked down the hill toward them.

"Sarge, what's going on, what are you—" His words were cut off when a red splotch appeared on his forehead, followed up by the crack of a gunshot. His jaw slackened, he fell to his knees, and collapsed forward.

"Well, this just got easier," Sergeant Fellyn said. "Bubbles was the last dumbass patriot in my group. Now I just gotta plug your gunner and the rest'll be easy to convince. CAPP paradise is waiting."

"Speak of the devil, Sarge," Klein said. She heard BDA shout and glanced up to see him through the trees. The sergeant took a shot and BDA dove behind a tree for cover.

While her two assailants focused on her gunner, she released a knife she'd folded up in her right fist. She flicked it across the gap in Klein's body armor above his right thigh. Surprised, he let go of her left hand to focus on the knife hand. In a rapid, fluid movement, she drew the carbon fiber blade from her belt and slashed Fellyn's wrist. He immediately released his grip on her throat. Spinning, she stabbed the knife quickly into Klein's side and then, before he could react to that, drove the sword flat along his chest and up into his jaw. With the strength of her entire body beneath her, she buried the blade into his skull. It stuck and she let go. Klein's corpse tumbled backwards.

In a blur, she dropped, drew another knife from her boot, and spun back to face Fellyn. He flipped the shotgun to bear, and she lunged left. A bullet cracked across his back, a present from BDA, and Fellyn instinctively tossed a glance up the hill.

One of her knives shot up, dug into the exoskeleton joint on the outside of his elbow, and cut the wiring. He fired, but she'd used his own arm to push the barrel away and it went wide. Shouting with rage, she slashed his calf with the other knife, popped up, jabbed his side, and, finally, drove the knife deep into his right armpit. The shotgun dropped with a thud into the dirt.

He dropped his weight, twisted, and raised his shoulder as he was trying to use his right arm, but it lacked the strength. She rolled the knife around his arm, pressed it against his neck, and dragged him off of his feet.

"Full of surprises," he gurgled as he fell backward. He struggled to move either arm, but she pressed the blade tighter to his throat.

"I left out my fourth rule," she said softly into his ear while catching her breath. He fought some more, and she dug the blade deep enough to draw blood. "Well, the first, really. You don't survive the world I grew up in if you can't gut whoever tries to take more than you're willing to give."

His weight shifted and she knew he was preparing to make a move.

"Guts," he smiled pathetically. "That's the nickname I should've asked about."

"Yeah," she replied. "*Guts*, because this little pilot *guts* men like you. But slitting a throat is just as good."

His arm flew up to grab her, but she drew the knife across his neck before he could. Renee pushed him forward and backed away as the blood spurted and bubbled out.

"Traitor!" she heard Keebler yell as he sprinted down the hill toward her.

"Keebler, no!" Trick said, half a step behind him. He caught up and tackled Keebler to the ground. The two hit the ground and sent up a cloud of dirt. "Sarge was the traitor, don't you get it?"

"He's right, Keebler," Private Szrebiec came down the hill now as well. "He killed our lieutenant. I didn't want to admit it, or, rather, I was afraid to say it out loud, but he did. He or Klein probably killed Li and Peters too."

"He just told me as much," Renee said, still sitting on the ground a few feet from the dead sergeant. "He wanted to surrender to the CAPP."

She gauged their reactions. Keebler and Beggar seemed lost in thought, as if they weighed the options. Trick ground his teeth in anger. BDA calmly stalked behind her and retrieved the pistol, ready to shoot any of them if they threatened her.

"He told me that the Chief doesn't care about us," she said as she gently climbed to her feet. "He said that the world I grew up in was proof. Where people destroy each other to survive. Where the weak are prey and the strong take charge."

"I agree, actually," Renee said. Their eyes narrowed at her words. "The country we're fighting for *has* gotten sick. Weak men have made times hard, but it's all part of the cycle. It gives people like you and me the chance to get strong. So we can fix what's wrong with our country. But we can't do that if we die here."

"The sergeant there," she gestured to the corpse, "and Daddy's boy over there, are the weak. The cowards. For a little safety and security, they would've betrayed their countrymen." The resolve in their eyes stiffened. Her speech had the effect she intended. It was time to drive it home.

"To the CAPP and everyone in the world, Americans are soft, lazy crybabies who can't fight. Time and again, we prove them wrong. Right now, I'm going to that missile site to prove them wrong again. I'm going to get those demo charges I lugged all this way and blow up what I can. I could use your help, but I'm doing it either way. We take out those SAMs, I make a call on SARSat, and who knows? Maybe the higher ups will be ready to send in a rescue package. If not, we keep moving until they do." She stalked off up the hill and didn't wait for them to follow.

"I know, guys, I know," BDA said as she walked away. "Officers, right?" He shrugged. "Anyway, let's go blow shit up."

Thunder Run

By J.F. Holmes

Eleven years post invasion

In the distance, Sergeant First Class Lisa Dash, Confederate Earth Forces, could see the outline of the broken Space Needle, lit by the setting moon. Though Seattle had taken a number of orbital strikes, the Invy had concentrated on hitting the numerous military bases instead of civilian populace. Joint Base Lewis-McChord (JBLM), Whidbey Island Naval Air Station, Kitsap, and Everett had all taken a pounding, even the Boeing manufacturing facilities. Except for a small area of JBLM that the Invy used to house a mechanized platoon, all their local forces were concentrated at the old SeaTac airport. The runway there was long enough that their cargo lifters— massive multi engine ships assisted by antigravity—could get a boost lifting off, carrying the loot of Earth.

The Confederate Earth Forces attack was scheduled to coincide with the submarines' firing on the orbital stations. Dash knew that if it worked, then they had a chance. If it didn't, well, no matter what their efforts amounted to, it was all over. A devout Catholic, she said a quick Hail Mary as they reached the last hill before their final run into the base and came to a stop in defilade. Behind the four tanks, three Bradley Fighting Vehicles and a half dozen wheeled Strykers were spread out, carrying the Main Force infantry soldiers of the 1-161st Infantry, the Highlanders. The runway at SeaTac was about ten miles away, through the ruins of the suburbs of Seattle. The men and women in the infantry were going to be advancing over ruins that had been, once, their homes.

The movements had been timed so that minutes before each orbital passed overhead, the armor came to a squeaking halt, cooling sprays venting their excess engine heat. That problem had taken a long time to solve, and the chemicals used in the dispersal were some really bad shit. The VA would probably deny their claims when they all died of cancer in a few years, Dash mused to herself as she idly sat watching the countdown.

Behind them, about three miles to the rear, crewmembers were slowly placing their hands on elevation wheels, getting ready to start engines to provide hydraulic power and silently screwing Variable Timed fuses on 155 caliber artillery rounds. Artillery, as mobile as it was had done little good against the first invasion, but here it was to keep the Invy's heads down while the tanks advanced. The six surviving Paladins of the 2nd Battalion, 146th Field Artillery Regiment had firing solutions for every square meter of the base. The howitzers had been fielded a week before, step by step, hiding from orbitals, going places the Invy patrols ignored.

Scout Team Eleven, four miles closer to the base, watched through night vision as an Invy foot patrol made its way out of the perimeter. On any other night, the scouts would have quietly slipped away, gathering information on times and routes, but not tonight. Each member of the seven man team held one of the Invy in their sights and would fire the first suppressed shots of the early morning.

The battle, like any combined arms battle, would be a dance carefully coordinated by the Regimental Commander. Timing was everything and Dash had the plan memorized in her head, but the veteran knew that it would all go out the window as soon as the dance started.

At H-Minus thirty seconds radio sets with pre-programmed, semi-intelligent software started broadcasting back and forth, all across the Puget Sound area, simulating a massive wave of communications traffic. An orbital had just crested the horizon; the hope was that the Invy would be unable to discern the real chatter from the fake and be overwhelmed by targets. Some radio sets were stationary, while others moved on small wheeled drones.

At H-Minus fifteen seconds, Dash turned on her radio in time to hear the Regimental Commander call, *"Execute and Godspeed, Rifle Six, out."* At the same moment, she felt the rumble of artillery fire in the soles of her boots as it slightly shook the seventy-ton tank. The rounds passing overhead made their characteristic ripping sound, and she hit the lever dropping her back into the tank, pulling the hatch shut after her and activating her helmet-mounted display. External sensors, modeled off the F-35 program, seemed to make the tank around her invisible, showing her a three hundred and sixty degree view of the outside, turning night into day.

"KICK IT, BITCH!" she yelled, half to the driver and half to the tank and Private First Class Terry Banks twisted the grip, engaging the drive. Dizzy Lehmkuhl already had her helmet mounted display going and the turret tracked side to side as she looked for targets, following the movement of her head. The big Canadian Corporal, Jamie Ibson, sat ready, his job the least high tech of all, set to open the door with his knee switch, select whatever round his commander asked for, and muscle it into the breech. A HEAT round was already loaded, giving them the best option against any targets they might face.

They were all thrown backwards by the acceleration and could hear Banks give a "whoop!" of joy as they tore down the highway. One thing that the engineers had never really overcome was the rough ride of any tracked vehicle, and on top of that, the highway was full of debris. There was a discernible lane through the wreckage, though; the Main Force soldiers had spent the last nine years surreptitiously moving them around to provide a semi-clear lane.

Behind the lead tank *Bad Bitch* came her sisters, *Orca, Suzie Q, Selchie,* and *Balrog.* Each had their guns aimed to one side or another, covering their sectors. Dash took a second to look behind her, her chest swelling with pride.

Finally, finally, finally.

The sixth vehicle in their column was their air defense, a bigger version of the EMP generator the ODA teams had. It crested the hill, lit up its radar, and immediately started knocking drones out of the sky. After ten seconds, the firing stopped, and the Stryker vehicle moved out again.

The Abrams reached a bone-jarring speed, crashing over piles of rubble and through ditches, the stabilized main gun tilting up and down in time with Lehmkuhl's aiming point. Dash was to draw first blood. She was scanning in a counterpoint motion to her gunner's and caught a glimpse of a shape starting to lift into the sky. Slapping the joystick into her hand, she overrode Lehmkuhl's sight, yelled, "FROM MY POSITION, AIRCRAFT, ON THE WAY!", flipped a switch that set the fuse to 'proximity', and triggered the gun.

The cannon lurched backwards, causing an enormous flash that lit the night, accompanied by an incredibly loud *CRACK* as the HEAT round ripped through the air.

Sergeant First Class Lisa Dash thought for a brief moment of her childhood in poverty, leaving Jamaica to come to America, how she had earned her college degree through serving in the Washington Army National Guard and how she built her own business and family—a husband and two daughters. All that had been torn from her; now, hellbent on revenge, she threw back her head and laughed as the round intercepted the flight path of the Invy ship. A second tank also fired, and the wingman peeled off east, leaving a glowing trail of sparks that, after a few seconds, erupted into a blinding flash of antimatter annihilation.

Lisa Dash laughed on and on, consumed by the joy of revenge as they pulled into their first pre-sighted firing position.

"RELOAD, SABOT!" Dash yelled, the laughter still continuing in her head. Ibson already had the door open, and his fingers punched the selector, making the bottom of the round pop outwards. He hauled mightily with his right hand on the base and his left on the top, then flipped it around, smoothly ramming it into the open mouth of the gun, then pulling his hand away as the heavy steel breech swung closed.

"UP!" he yelled, and Dizzy yelled "ON THE WAY!" The gun rocked backwards, the tank with it, pushing it down onto its springs. Dash could have demanded that the gunner run through the standard fire commands, but she trusted Dizzy Lehmkuhl to do a good job keeping them alive. Ibson didn't wait for a command either: from here on out it was sabot until either the gunner or the commander ordered differently. Fine by him.

"Driver, back up!" she ordered, as return fire started to come their way. Their opposition was a company of Invy tanks—if their crews managed to get to them before the artillery cut them down. She had to assume they would face the full dozen the Invy organized their companies in, though. The Abrams dropped backwards, and she started to give the driver commands to maneuver them to the next spot when the left side of her vision temporarily whited out, and an explosion rocked *Bad Bitch* sideways on her tracks.

A hundred meters away the turret of *Suzie Q* leapt upward into the air, flipped over twice and then fell back on top of the hull, almost snuffing out the fire that raged inside. The track commander, less experienced than Dash, had let his driver expose the shot trap, the space between the hull and the turret, while scanning for targets. A100mm plasma bolt had blown through the drivers' head, under the main gun, across the loader, and hit the anti-matter reactor that drove the tank. The resulting explosion had come back into the crew compartment and vented its fury in that confined space, incinerating the crew and lifting the forty-ton turret high into the air.

She had no time to mourn her friends, only to fight the tanks. They were to engage at long distance, draw the enemies' fire while the infantry swung wide around the base. It could be that tonight, they weren't going to get out of here alive, but she'd take some of the bastards with her. *Bad Bitch* rolled fifty meters west, shielded by the hill, and then moved through the ruin of a house, the muzzle of her gun being given a narrow view to scan.

Lehmkuhl caught a glimpse of the angular side of an Invy tank also shifting position, rotating on its air cushion. She fired, and the sabot round punched through the skirts. The Invy vehicle bounced backwards and settled on the ground, but the plasma cannon started to rotate in their direction.

Dash yelled at the driver to back up, but the gunner yelled, "HOLD!" even as Ibson raced to load the gun. The commander was tempted to kick Lehmkuhl in the head for countermanding her order, but settled on triggering the .50 caliber from her position, hoping the tracer fire and impacts would distract the Invy gunner.

With a *HISS-CRACK* and a charge of static, the plasma bolt scored the top of the turret, melting a groove and overloading the active camouflage. Lehmkuhl fired a second later, the sabot arching out and crashing through the engine of the Invy tank, a small spark followed by an explosion that was so bright it shone through the metal.

Ibson turned to load another round, but Dash shouted, "HEAT, APC, FROM MY POSITION!" Two seconds later Ibson yelled, "UP!" and the commander fired, knocking out an Invy Armored Personnel Carrier that had been crossing the runway.

"All Rifles, general advance," came over the radio and Banks, listening in, didn't wait for the order. She applied full torque to the drive wheels, and *Bad Bitch* charged forward, main gun swinging to and fro, searching for targets. On her left *Orca* and *Selchie* followed, barely visible, but *Balrog* was silent and still, a smoking wreck. while *Suzie Q* continued to burn like a blowtorch.

From the sky, orbital fired rods began to pound down all around the Seattle area, but the radio distractions seemed to be working. For some reason, no one at the base was adjusting fire onto their attack, and Dash was grateful for it. Lehmkuhl let off a snap shot at an Invy tank trying to maneuver west towards the mechanized infantry, who they must have sighted. The Invy's turret bounced upward a foot then settled back—the vehicle, now immobile, crashed into the side of a building. The gunner swept the Invy with the coax as they drove past, and *Orca* took out another a kilometer away. Artillery rained down on the base, cratering the runway and shattering the control tower, starting fires.

On her HUD (heads-up display), targets marked by the infantry started to appear as red icons, but Dash ignored them.

The display then lit up with a live video feed from a UAV launched in the air from the artillery positions. It only lasted for fifteen seconds before a plasma bolt swept it from the sky, but it was enough to see the hot spots of the three remaining Invy tanks, clustered around the corner of the control tower, shielded from direct artillery fire by the building. Someone was going to have to dig them out. To the left were a ragged line of infantry, Wolverines who, despite the surprise and ferocity of the attack, were dug in and hammering effective shots at the human dismounts.

"Orca," she called over the radio, "go help the dismounts." Her captain was a smear of jelly inside the belly of *Balrog*, so Dash was now in command of the three element unit. "*Selchie*, I'm going to make a thunder run past their position to get their attention. You come in right behind me, make it quick and make it count."

"You got it," came back immediately, and Dash switched over to the intercom.

"Terry, how fast can you make the bitch go?" she asked the driver.

"No idea, but we're gonna find out!" responded Banks. Locked in her driver's coffin, she had no way of knowing that eight of her friends were dead.

"Punch it, then!"

The seventy-ton Abrams, driven by antimatter hellfire, leapt forward. The turret, rotating as they accelerated forward, struggled to keep up with Lehmkuhl's fixed gaze at the corner of the building. When they hit the opening, crossing in front of the three waiting Invy tanks, *Bad Bitch* was going almost ninety miles an hour, the tracks threatening to fly apart at the slightest deviation from a straight line. The first two Invy tanks didn't have the reaction time to fire at her as she sped past, but the third let go just as *Bad Bitch*'s cannon fired point blank into it.

The Invy tank exploded in a thunderous roar, shoving the other two off to one side, but not before the plasma bolt hit *Bad Bitch* in her forward skirt. Her left track blew apart in a shower of glowing steel fragments, the plasma continuing through the hull, cutting Banks's legs off at the knees before exiting out the other side.

The tank skidded sideways, losing momentum and power at the same time, and all three of the crew were thrown forward. Dash smashed her face into the commander's sight, cracking the HUD and knocking her senseless. She crumpled and slid off her seat, on top of Dizzy.

Dizzy had seen the shit coming and leaned into the wall of the tank at the last second, crushing her against it but not injuring her. She was hurt more by Dash falling on her than anything else. In the adrenaline rush, she didn't notice the large piece of heavy duty wire sticking out of her abdomen, but when she did, the gunner went pale with shock. Then she bit down hard on her lip, drawing blood and willed the injury out of her mind.

"Gimme…gimme a SITREP…" muttered Dash, but then she followed it with a mumbled, "Johnson, I need a charge five and level that damn gun…" Lehmkuhl knew that she was someplace else, some other when-else and useless. She gently moved her boss aside, trying to ignore the screams coming from the trapped driver.

"Jamie, reload sabot and poke your head out, tell me what's going on!" she hissed urgently, and the Canadian shook his head to clear it. He manually slid the ammo doors back and loaded a sabot round, muttered "up", then carefully lifted his hatch a few inches. All the sensors were dead, and it was back to the human eye.

"Jesus!" Jamie said, "All three Invy are done, *Selchie*'s blown all to hell, and holy shit, there's one more maneuvering around the wrecks! And I think that's *Orca* burning on the other side! Fucker's going after the infantry, he's going to eat them for lunch!" The stress and smoke made his voice harsh.

"Get down here and crank the turret!" she yelled, flipping her sight over to manual and pressing her face to it.

The big Canadian slid back down and grabbed at the manual traverse, grunting as he furiously spun the wheel. The compartment was filling up with smoke, and Banks's screams stopped abruptly. They were followed a moment later by the muffled bark of a pistol shot, and Ibson squeezed his eyes shut as he worked. "Goodbye, Terry," he mumbled.

"Faster, dammit!" Jamie didn't answer Lehmkuhl; his arm was growing tired, and he was close to passing out from the fumes. The red emergency lighting and smoke was turning the place into a vision of hell. Suddenly an automated female voice began to blare, "REACTOR CRITICAL, REACTOR CRITICAL" in a flat, dispassionate tone.

Unaware of the puddle of blood growing on the floor beneath her, Dizzy Lehmkuhl watched the side skirts of the enemy tank creep into her vision. Closer…closer… The world began to fade to black around the edges of her vision. *Good enough*, she thought and squeezed the trigger.

The 120mm gun jumped backwards, and the Invy tank seemed to spin sideways. Then, a shower of sparks erupted from the main hull, and it settled down, lifeless and smoking.

The gunner slumped forward over her sight, then rolled against the breech and lay still.

Corporal Ibson reached down, grabbed Sergeant Dash by the deadman's strap on the back of her coveralls and heaved. Her slight frame rose up, and he shoved her out of the loader's hatch. Then he grabbed Lehmkuhl around the waist and manhandled her up, appalled by the amount of blood soaking the front of her uniform.

"Come on, Dizzy, stay with me!" he muttered, trying to get her dead weight out, when a pair of hands reached in and grabbed at her body and pulled her through. Brass from his own 240B machine gun showered down through the open hatch, but he couldn't hear the shots over the screeching of the warning system.

He pulled himself out to see two crewmen from *Selchie*: one manning the gun, hammering shots at distant enemy infantry, and the other helping Sergeant Dash stumble away towards the other side of the runway. Ibson hit the other man in the shoulder to let him know he was out, but caught up in the madness of battle, he was ignored. A plasma bolt glanced off the turret and blew his head off, showering Ibson with superheated blood. Ibson picked up Lehmkuhl's body gently in his arms, slid down the side of *Bad Bitch* and ran.

What a hell of a way to go! thought *Bad Bitch*, and she managed to wait fifteen more seconds until the Invy infantry had swarmed around her. Then she erupted in a flash of light as the antimatter containment module ruptured. If a tank had a soul, she joined her friends on Fiddlers' Green.

It's one thing to face a battle with seventy tons of metal around you. It's a whole different experience to have nothing between you and a hissing bolt of plasma but a few layers of Kevlar and nylon.

Ibson barely made it to the edge of the runway with Lehmkuhl when their world was filled with unholy light and a crushing wave knocked her out of his arms, throwing them both down into the ditch. Then there was deafening silence, punctuated only with the sounds of ammunition cooking off.

"Gotta get back in the fight! Goddamned clinks are ever what go!" yelled Dash, making no sense. She started to stand up, then stumbled. The crewman from the *Selchie* pulled her back down and laid on top of her to stop her from struggling.

Ibson ignored her for the moment, ripping at the Velcro of Lehmkuhl's vest, then unzipping her coveralls all the way down to her waist. The piece of braided wire, a quarter of an inch thick, had slipped under the vest, punched through the tough nylon and under her ribs. Her whole front was soaked with blood, her belly swollen with internal bleeding, and she looked deathly pale in the glow of the burning control tower.

"Come on, Dizzy, don't do this to me!' he muttered and felt for a pulse. It was there, but really weak and erratic. He lifted her eyelid and saw that her pupils had rolled upwards, barely showing. Not fucking good. He wrapped a compression bandage around her waist, covering the wound, and elevated her legs. Then he turned to the other man who was dealing with Sergeant Dash and said, "Can you keep her down?"

"I dunno, dude, she's really out of it. Keeps babbling about killing Chinese."

"Okay, I'll be right back," said Ibson and he stood, glanced around and ran across the runway.

"Where are you going?"

"To find a medkit," Ibson replied. Plasma fire started from another building a hundred meters away, tracking towards him and then a heavier, automatic weapon chased after the Canadian, making him run faster than he thought he ever could in his life. One almost clipped his boot as he dove behind the smoking wreck of *Selchie*, he paused a moment to catch his breath as plasma arced and spit off the hull.

The tank had died with her gun pointing directly at an Invy tank, the turret turned sideways. He knew the soldier helping Dash was *Selchie*'s loader, and he had recognized the one killed at the machine gun as her commander. The driver and gunner had probably died inside the turret, but as he looked up, he saw the commander's hatch was open.

Counting out loud, when he reached three, he ran around the side of the tank, grabbed a rail and vaulted up onto the hull. Before the Invy could zero in on him, Ibson slipped in face first through the hatch, landing on the commander's seat upside down.

The smoke immediately made him start coughing; the emergency red lighting, smell of charred flesh and fried blood made the place seem like some circle of Dante's inferno. The driver sat in her seat, missing her bottom half, eyes wide open and staring. The gunner, who had been a good friend of his, slowly cooked as hydraulic fluid dripped onto his mangled body, feeding a small fire. Ibson tried to breathe, but the smell of roasted human flesh overcame him, and he threw up violently. Struggling to turn himself upright, his hands found the medkit he was looking for, unsnapped it from the wall, and he weakly pulled himself out of the hatch, rolled over and fell ten feet to the pavement.

He landed on his arm and there was a sickening *SNAP* at his wrist, but he gritted his teeth and stood up, slung the medkit across his body and tried to peek out around the right side of the tank. Plasma fire hammered at him so fast he almost lost this head; the Wolverines had zeroed on him, waiting for him to come back. He was stuck and Dizzy needed him, ASAP.

Screw it. Ibson launched himself out onto the runway, running even faster than he had before. Halfway across, he fell flat, and a burst of fire sheeted over him, the heavy machine gun having waited for him. In a flash, he stood back up and ran again, diving into the ditch and screaming with pain as he slid down the slope.

"Help me!" he yelled, trying to open the medkit one handed. The other soldier made a quick decision, got up off Dash and helped Ibson open the medkit. Before Dash could get up again, the soldier grabbed a shot of morphine and went back to the disoriented Jamaican.

Ibson quickly found the package of nanos, jabbed the button marked "INTERNAL BLEEDING", waited two seconds, opened it, then jabbed the needle directly into Lehmkuhl's abdomen. She quickly started to convulse, then went rigid, breath heaving in and out. There was one more thing he could do: he quickly slipped an IV into her veins, which were in danger of collapsing, got the needle in after three tries and squeezed the plasma into her until the bag was empty.

Ibson's next move was to shoot an orange pen flare a hundred feet up into the air, calling for a medevac. Ibson had no idea how the rest of the battle was going; heavy automatic weapons fire and plasma cracks sounded in the distance, but the ones that had been shooting at him on the runway had grown quiet. Too quiet.

A suggestion of movement at the far end of the ditch in the dim moonlight drew his attention, and he hissed a warning to the other soldier, whose name he couldn't remember. They both drew their pistols, and Ibson laid down in front of

Lehmkuhl, shielding her body with his. The movement resolved into a squad of Wolverines who approached them quietly: six of them led by a Dragon. Half the lesser Invy had their ripper claws extended and the Dragon leaked blood all over its gold armor but smiled with razor sharp teeth.

Ibson and the soldier nodded to each other and raised their pistols. They were dead men, but they knew they had beaten the Invy if the Dragon was fleeing the Command Center. Fuck it. They had won. It was kind of bittersweet, to have come so far, but…

Thirty tons of Bradley Fighting Vehicle crashed over the side of the ditch and into the Invy squad, knocking them down like bowling pins. The driver ground the tracks back and forth, spinning the vehicle first one way then the next, grinding the stunned Invy into a red paste of skin, snapped bones, and raw meat.

One of the Wolverines had escaped the collision, and the two men emptied their pistols into it from ten meters away, firing until their slides locked back. The Bradley stopped and the turret rotated, hammering out thunderous three round bursts even as the back ramp slammed down. Before it did, Ibson saw a crude green and black painting of a long necked animal spitting plasma and knew it was one of Alpha Companies' Brads, nicknamed "Attack Llama". The infantry squad leader directed two of his men to help the wounded to the track; they quickly strapped Lehmkuhl onto a stretcher and carried her inside.

The rest joined the main gun in firing towards the buildings, then at some unseen signal, the firing stopped, and they all dashed back into the track. As the ramp whirred up, they were thrown violently to one side, and then the Brad started back down the runway towards the impromptu aid station a mile away. One man struggled to strap Dash into a seatbelt, and she fought wildly, despite the morphine, then slumped and lay still, a spray of blood leaking out of her nose. The man put his fingers to her neck, searching for a pulse, looked at his NCO and shook his head.

In the battle lighting, Ibson could see that every man there, even the ones who had dismounted and continued fighting, was badly wounded or burned. The squad leader leaned over and yelled in Ibson's ear, "You guys really saved our asses! Where's the rest of the tank crews?"

The Canadian said nothing in answer, just reached over and held Lehmkuhl's bloody, slightly warm hand in his. Then he put his other hand over his face and great, wracking sobs convulsed his body. The infantryman next to him put his arm around Ibson's neck and the tanker laid his head on his shoulder, still bleeding silent tears.

No one said anything for the rest of the short ride.

Breach Of Contract

By William Joseph Roberts

2683 AD / 140 years post-Terran Accords & cessation of Galactic Civil War
Day 21, Delz-Tik Deployment / 1349 Local Time
Eastern range of the Barris Mountains, Delz-Tik Industries Expeditionary Claim Zone
Hopkins Moon orbiting Haedus 5, Outer Rim of the Perseus arm

"I don't think these shit-stains heard you, Mongo," Lieutenant "Doc" Amison said with a chuckle over the secure comm channel.

"Or they're ignoring me," Captain Todd "Mongo" Dillon replied. Adjusting course, he let the heavy AH1C-AV34 Hellcat gunship slip sideways. He kept the nose of the hovering craft pointed at the approaching convoy, a mix of Armored Personnel Carriers and ground transports. "You'd think a pair of Fulcrums and a Hellcat hanging overhead would be enough to give these guys the hint that they aren't welcome."

Doc laughed over their channel. "You'd sure think so. And that's after the Jacks battalion wiped two platoons of these asshats off the face of this stupid little moon. Let me and the boys squeeze off a few rounds in their general direction. That might get their attention." Doc's Fulcrum hovered a few hundred feet off their starboard side mirrored by Warrant Officer Alan "Rabbit" Goodspeed's Fulcrum a few hundred feet off to their port side.

The Fairchild Republic FR-AX Fulminus II split-wing VTOL spaceplanes were some mean-looking and combat-proven craft.

Capable of carrying four Infernus ground attack missiles and CB-C Oculi Petram cluster bombs, plus the integral Executor EXE-72 multi-barreled laser cannon and a 20mm Gauss cannon mounted near the end of each of the four wings. The crafts rightfully struck fear into most opponents that found themselves facing off against them.

"Come on, please Cap," Staff Sergeant "Pluto" Brown begged. "I haven't had a chance to test-fire the Barts since I rebuilt them."

Mongo glanced back through the cockpit access hatch into the main hold where Sergeant Brown manned one of the ship's three Barts; a Dane-Arms eight-barreled 12.7mm Gatling Gauss turret stationed at the Hellcat's open starboard side door. "Don't forget to turn on your O2, Pluto. The thin atmosphere sneaks up on you before you know it. I don't need you getting dizzy from hypoxia and falling out the side of the ship. That's just more paperwork for Doc to fill out."

"Oh, I see how it is," Doc grumbled. "Just cause he's my second brother's cousin means I get stuck dealing with him?"

"No," Mongo said. "It's because I really hate doing paperwork and I outrank you. Rank does have its privileges at times."

"Dammit!" Private "Brick" Johnson broke in over the comms. "I knew I'd forgotten something."

"You alright back there, Brick?" Mongo asked.

"Yeah, just forgetting the stupid stuff like turning on my oxygen."

"Don't worry kid," Pluto chimed in. "If you fall out and kill yourself, Doc can do your paperwork too."

Riotous laughter filled the comms.

Mongo adjusted his own mask and did a quick check of his oxygen flow. "Alright, spaz down," Mongo ordered. "We still have a job to do if we want to get paid, ladies." He keyed the open frequency on the radio. "I repeat. Unknown convoy, this is Captain Todd Dillon of the Fifth Expeditionary Air Combat Brigade. State your intentions and identify yourselves."

"Sure would be nice to make some extra cash for a change," Doc added. "The last two garrison patrol gigs have barely covered my drinking habit."

Mongo laughed. "If I understood the Colonel correctly, there's a hefty bonus involved if these corporate assholes find what they're looking for."

"What exactly is it that they're after?" Brick asked.

"Old Empire tech from what I heard," Doc added.

"But," Brick said questioningly, "why would they think they'll find anything way out here?"

Mongo grunted. "It's all about Old Empire technology per the brief I got when we arrived."

Pluto grunted. "I heard that some Takan survey team found a couple of Old Empire frigates and some sort of repair yard. Next thing you know a boom town springs up overnight on the ass end of the galaxy."

"You're talking about Hub Town, aren't you?"

"Yup. Have you been there yet?"

"No," Brick said.

Pluto laughed. "We'll have to remedy that. You haven't lived until you've witnessed the Clu'lacan basket dance put on by the hookers down at the Hub Town whore house."

"Eh hem," Mongo interrupted. "Remember the convoy?"

"Oh yeah," Pluto said with a chuckle.

"Let me give the lead vehicle one little pop across their nose like you'd do any dumb-assed dog," Rabbit added, breaking into the conversation.

Mongo slowed the speed of his flanking maneuver and kept pace with the two other ships. Clouds of dust kicked up from the desert below as Rabbit hovered in his Fulcrum fifty feet off the deck at the Hellcat's ten o'clock. Doc maintained his Fulcrum to the Hellcat's two o'clock as the trio continued circling the moving convoy.

"What's the call, Mongo?" Doc asked.

Mongo let out a reluctant sigh. "Hold fire. Let's give them one last chance." Mongo keyed the open frequency once more. "I repeat to the unauthorized vehicle convoy, you have entered the active claim zone of Delz-Tik Industries Incorporated. Deadly force is authorized to maintain claim security per the Trade Confederation Hopkins Expedition Accords. Return to Hub Town immediately or you *will* be fired upon."

Tracer rounds streamed out from the lead APC as it opened fire.

"Shit!" Doc shouted over the team frequency. "I think you got their attention, Cap!" Doc gunned his throttle and swung his Fulcrum clear of the fire as Mongo squeezed the trigger on the Hellcat's control stick. The twin wingtip mounted 20mm Gauss cannons thundered to life, pulverizing the forward section of the lead APC.

"Fuck yes!" Pluto shouted. "God I love the smell of scorched ozone in the morning! Oorah motherfuckers!" Pluto unleashed his own taste of hell across the convoy in the form of 12.7mm Gauss rounds that cut a path of destruction down the line of vehicles.

The remainder of the APCs in the convoy took evasive action and followed suit, opening fire on the hovering gunships.

"What are you waiting for, Rabbit? Light them up," Mongo ordered.

"My fire control system is FUBAR. I've got nothing, Cap. Hard reset didn't even work."

"Then get your ass clear…"

A concealed weapons point appeared on the roof of the rearmost APC. Mongo didn't have the chance to finish his sentence before the APC fired, striking Rabbit's Fulcrum on the underbelly with a small-caliber artillery round as he attempted to veer the craft away from the firefight.

Rabbit's Fulcrum bucked from the impact and rolled. Falling from the sky, it disappeared behind a large dune to their east.

"Sweet fucking baby Jesus! That son of a bitch just greased the FNG."

"Rabbit is down," Mongo shouted into the comms. "I repeat, Rabbit is down!"

"I see him," Doc replied as he lined his Fulcrum up for a strafing run across the convoy. "Fulcrum looks intact. He bellied her in on the backside of that dune." Lasers flashed from the nose of Doc's Fulcrum as the Executor Gatling laser pulsed, leaving a line of faint scorch marks across the top of the rear APC. "These guys are running ablative armor, Cap. I barely scratched the surface of the caboose."

"What the hell!" Pluto shouted between trigger pulls. The concussion of the Barts' 12.7mm burst fire quaked the thin air inside the Hellcat's cabin. "Rabbit owes me twenty creds!"

"Not anymore he doesn't," Brick added.

"Shut it, shit-brick! If that son of a bitch is dead, I'm gonna bring his ass back and kill him myself. He ain't getting out of paying me that easy!" Pluto unleashed a ten-second burst of fire from the door-mounted gun that ripped through the vehicle like a laser torch, detonating a munition it must have been transporting. Small bits of debris rained down for at least fifty meters surrounding the crater where the transport had just been.

"These guys aren't fucking around, are they?" Doc said.

"Doesn't look like it," Mongo replied. "These claim jumpers are just getting worse the longer we're on this rock."

Mongo activated the Hellcat's belly-mounted heavy laser turret and targeted the convoy's last remaining APC as it broke from the line and fled southwest across cold desert badlands. With a flash, a molten hole of slag the size of a man's fist sluffed away from the rear of the vehicle followed by a dozen more that chewed their way across the vehicle's armored roof. The APC suddenly jinked left and slid sideways off the edge of the hard-packed soil down an embankment.

"That armor may have held up to your pulse laser, Doc, but it didn't like the feel of the heavy." Mongo allowed the Hellcat to slide sideways, circling the APC as it tumbled down the hillside.

"Score one for the good guys," Doc said. "That's what four times the power output will do for you."

Pluto chuckled then let out an ear-piercing, "Yee Haw," and squeezed off another burst of fire from his Bart. "Oorah!"

"Cut the chatter and save the ammo," Mongo ordered. He swung the Hellcat around, aiming for the downed Fulcrum. "DTI Base Camp, this is Right-Hand Lead."

"This is DTI Base Camp, we copy you, Right-Hand Lead. Go ahead Mongo."

"Mission complete. Rabbit is down. Moving in for recovery. Requesting a Rhino for extraction of the Fulcrum and anything salvageable from the convoy."

"Copy that, Mongo. Scrambling Bender and his Rhino with a medevac crew. ETA, twenty minutes."

Mongo let out a long sigh. "I copy, Base Camp. Right-Hand out." He lowered the landing gear and eased the Hellcat down onto the loose desert floor near the downed Fulcrum.

"Hey kid, you ever seen a dead body?" Pluto shouted over to Brick as he secured his Bart into the stowage cradle.

"No," Brick replied, a light quaver to his voice.

Pluto hit the release on his O2 mask then pulled a wad of tobacco from a pouch and shoved it into his cheek. He chewed for a moment before spitting a stream of viscous brown out the transport's door and flashing a wide, tobacco-brown smile at the private. "Well, there's a first time for everything." He grabbed his tool bag and hopped out the side of the Hellcat.

2683 AD / 140 years post-Terran Accords & cessation of Galactic Civil War
Day 22, Delz-Tik Deployment / 0600 Local Time
Delz-Tik Industries Expeditionary Base Camp
Eastern range of the Barris Mountains, Hopkins Moon

"Do I seriously need to reiterate *again* to you morons how important it is that you DO NOT BREAK MY EQUIPMENT?" Colonel Reggie Albeza shouted. A massive vein crossed the left side of his forehead and throbbed like it was about to explode. His thick black mustache gyrated like a weasel determined to mate with the colonel's upper lip as he chewed on the end of a large cigar.

"Rabbit is going to make a full recovery after his back heals," Doc interrupted. "That's something, isn't it?"

The colonel's fuming gaze turned in Doc's direction. "Pilots are a dime a dozen, or have you forgotten your place, Lieutenant?" He pounded a meaty fist down onto the long metal chow table that he leaned against. "I can replace the lot of you meat sacks ten times over for half of what it will cost to replace one Fulcrum." He glared down at Doc as he continued to chew on the end of his cigar. "We must maintain a ready fleet of functional warbirds in order to complete our contractual obligations. Do I need to remind you *dipshits* how hard it happens to be to get parts for the birds currently in our inventory?"

Pluto removed the lid of a caffeine ration bottle and let a mouthful of tobacco juice slide ever so indiscreetly into it. "How hard is that, Colonel?" Pluto asked, then adjusted his chew to the opposite cheek.

"Will someone please tell me why we keep your redneck ass around?"

"Because he's the best mechanic we have, sir," Mongo replied.

Pluto smiled wide. "You're just jealous that I'm better-looking than you." He slapped his own knee and let out a chuckle snort.

The colonel pulled the cigar from his mouth and pointed it in Pluto's direction. "You're damned lucky you're useful. Just as soon as you become dead weight, I'll cut you from the roster." His wild-eyed glare snapped around the room. "That goes for every damned one of you stick jockeys and knuckle draggers alike," he said, pointing his finger in a slow arc around the room. "I'll have every one of your sorry asses transferred to the Helia Prime deuterium mines for guard duty."

"Oh, we know," Mongo added. "You make sure to mention it almost daily, I think." He looked around at the others who nodded in agreement.

The colonel stared silently at Mongo, his mustache undulating as he thought through what was probably his next loving words of encouragement.

"Still isn't Rabbit's fault, sir," Doc said. "The kid got blindsided. Could have happened to any of us. He just happened to be the first one that fuck in the APC targeted."

"Be that as it may, Rabbit isn't off the hook yet. Until a full investigation can be completed, he may still be brought up on charges of negligence along with his trainer."

The room erupted in protest.

"What the hell! That's bullshit!" Mongo shouted. "His fire control malfunctioned."

"Doesn't matter, and you know it, Captain. There still has to be an investigation, so the corporate higher-ups holding our purse strings get their warm fuzzies from making my life miserable."

"Why are we even here, sir," Brick asked, breaking into the conversation. "I mean, shouldn't we be dealing with border disputes or quelling some sort of insurrections somewhere? I mean, how did we become corporate babysitters?"

"Because the corps are in bed with Terra Prime. Delz-Tik Industries is the best at retro engineering and recovery of retro-tech, and the government wants the technology for their own use if there is any technology to be had.

The colonel let out a growl then picked up the datapad laying on the table in front of him. "Now if you ladies are quite done, I'd like to wrap up this brief, so I can get to the mountain of paperwork Rabbit has caused me."

He scrolled through the list of assignments and barked a laugh before he looked up from the pad and smiled.

"I know that look," Doc said.

"It means someone is about to get screwed," Pluto added.

Mongo sighed. "Yup."

The colonel laughed. "Since I'm such a nice and forgiving person, I'm going to assign Bravo squad the inspection of Rabbit's Fulcrum."

"And here it comes," Doc said under his breath.

"Yup," Mongo agreed.

"We have received notification that a VIP has arrived in system on a Takan transport that will touch down at the Hub Town Starport sometime in the next six hours. The VIP is Dorian Vasquez, the CEO of Delz-Tik Industries. I'll assign Bravo squad to the task of inspecting Rabbit's Fulcrum while Mongo, Pluto, and Doc retrieve Mister Vasquez and escort him back to base camp."

"Sir, why is some corporate suit coming all the way out here to the ass end of the galaxy?"

"He came to inspect the progress that the dig team is making."

Pluto groaned. "I'd rather be covered head to toe in hydraulic fluid than to be stuck on a babysitting job."

Colonel Albeza's brows furrowed. He focused his glare toward Pluto then smiled.

"Mongo, Pluto, and Doc. Since you will be acting as dignitaries of the Fifth Brigade, and we want to make a very good impression on the man signing our very expensive paychecks for this expedition, I want each of you in your best. Full-service dress is mandatory for this assignment. Is that understood?"

The room erupted in a mixture of laughter and groans.

Pluto stood, holding his hand high over his head. "Can we at least take the FNG with us, Colonel? He hasn't had the opportunity to see what a boomtown is like."

Colonel Albeza chewed on his cigar for a moment in thought. "Sure. Knock yourselves out. But so help me if I find out that you've been fucking around and not keeping to the assignment, I'll dole out the corporal punishment myself," he said as he turned to leave. "Dismissed!"

2683 AD / 140 years post-Terran Accords & cessation of Galactic Civil War
Day 22, Delz-Tik Deployment / 1000 Local Time
Grilka's Lair / Hub Town / Hopkins Moon

Private Brick Johnson burst through the entrance hatch of Grilka's Lair, the only strip club and bar in Hub Town, and propped himself against the shipping container structure. He pushed his oxygen mask out of the way before he doubled over clenching his stomach. He let out a painful roar and projectile vomited its contents.

"Fucking new kids!" Doc shouted with a laugh.

"Without a doubt, Shit-Brick has got to be the sorriest FNG I have ever seen in my life," Pluto said as he exited the building. He squared his service cap on his head. "What's wrong, Shit-Brick? Do you need your mommy?" He tucked a wad of chew into his jaw, spit, then snapped his mask back into place.

Doc secured his own mask, then laughed. "I bet Madam Grilka would let him suckle on a tit or two for a few credits. It might be worth it if it helps to calm him down."

Brick gagged again at the thought of the hairy, four-armed Dandakaranya female and retched. The remainder of his breakfast splattered on the dusty ground.

"Or, maybe not," Doc continued. "Hey, to each their own, I guess. Genetic manipulations have their good sides and their bad. You just sometimes have to look past the bad to find the good. And did I not warn you that the Clu'lacan basket show would be a sight you'd never forget?" Pluto and Doc let out a riotous laugh. "You'd never think that a Clu'lacan could bend like that."

Mongo buttoned the double breast of his long service coat into place as he exited the structure. He choked on a short breath and remembered his mask before squaring up his own service cap. "You know if he pukes in the ship, you two are cleaning it up."

Pluto snorted a chuckle. "It's not our fault the kid has the stomach of some rainbow hugging nonner."

"I'm fine," Brick said as he stood and wiped his mouth before putting his mask on. He sucked down a few breaths then attempted to clear the bile from his mouth before securing it on his face. "I might need some brain bleach though. And it wasn't the basket show."

The other three looked at the young private with curious astonishment.

"Let's get to the starport before we're late," Mongo ordered. "Wouldn't want to disappoint the colonel."

Doc cleared his throat as he and the others fell in step with the captain. "So, what exactly was it that got you turning three shades of green, Private? Couldn't have been the human strippers. Stumpy might have been the exception there, but otherwise, they all looked like any other healthy human stripper that I've ever seen."

Pluto laughed. "Healthy is a relative term."

Color climbed up the sides of Brick's neck. "No, it wasn't any of them. They were more than gorgeous," he said in a shaky tone.

"Don't even think about trying to marry one of them," Doc said. "That's a bad idea all around no matter who you are."

"No, nothing like that," Brick continued. "It was the Takan fruit show on the other side of the room."

Pluto chuckled and let out a long sigh. "I remember my first time seeing that one. One hell of a night that I'll never forget. Szu Ming was her name if I remember right."

Mongo looked to Pluto with a look of concern. "Oh god. I hear a story coming on."

"Oh no, Cap. Nothing like that. Just basking in the warm memories of my first visit to Alpha Centauri is all."

"I have one question though," Brick said.

"Shoot, kid."

"Why were…" Brick suddenly stopped and gagged at the memory. "Why were those troopers catching the pieces in their mouths?" Brick gagged again.

"Oh! Them!" Pluto grunted in a low caveman-like tone. "We infantry. We bad. We kick ass, ug. Those retards are part of the 69th Infantry Platoon. The Ground Pounders unit. Grunts in the purest sense of the word. You don't have to be a genius to sign up with that unit, just willing to get shot at and charge into whatever shitshow the brass want to send you into."

"Bunch of over-rated bullet catchers if you ask me," Doc added.

"Oh, they are," Mongo agreed. "I flew transport for them as a butter bar lieutenant. They may be grunts, but they get the job done no matter what."

"And just look at you now," Pluto jibbed. "All grown up and pretty in your fancy new dress uniform. I bet your mamma sure is proud of you."

Mongo stopped and squared up with the Sergeant before quietly saying, "She very much is." He adjusted Pluto's hat to regulation, then turned and continued in the direction of the Hub Town starport. Several atmospheric transports slowly lifted off, bound for any number of destinations planetside.

Mongo stopped and looked around for the source of a loud rumble in the sky. Off to the south, he could see the bulky shape of a Takan heavy-lift transport as it rumbled in on approach. There was nothing sleek or sexy about the design of the GHC-922, the Terran designation for the transport. It looked like a flying tadpole with winglets and was meant to transport bulk cargo from remote mining outposts to the core worlds for processing. The only remarkable aspect of the craft was that it didn't need a jump gate to get around the galaxy. Even though it was painfully slow to recharge, the onboard jump system was effective at doing its job.

"If I had to guess," Mongo said to no one in particular, "that would probably be the transport that we're waiting for."

"You know exactly how to take the fun out of the party, don't you Cap?" Doc asked.

Mongo sighed. "Unfortunately, but we still have a job to do." He turned back to the others, giving them a quick once over. "I guess you apes look good enough to meet the man."

Doc adjusted the collar of his coat and brushed his sleeves. "You're damned right we are. We make this uniform look good, don't we boys?"

"Oorah!" they shouted with cheering laughter as they continued toward the starport through the dusty streets of Hub Town.

"I received a report prior to reaching orbit that your team lost an aircraft and a pilot," Dorian Vasquez said as he stepped through the side door of the Hellcat. He straightened his expensive-looking pin-striped suit, then fiddled with his uncomfortable oxygen mask. The overly tight straps of the mask dug into his face, leaving red pressure marks behind on his tanned skin.

"That's only partially true, Mister Vasquez." Mongo stepped into the cabin and motioned to a jump seat at the back of the cockpit. "If you'd prefer a seat with a view, you are more than welcome to join me up here instead of the drop troop racks in the cargo hold."

Vasquez smiled and straightened his tie. He nodded after a moment of thought. "That would be exciting. I think I will, Captain. Thank you."

Mongo slid into the pilot's seat and initiated the warm-up sequence. Auxiliary Power Units whined to life. Doc assisted the Delz-Tik CEO with securing himself into the small fold-down jump seat. The fuselage vibrated as the main engines rumbled to life.

Doc pulled the shoulder straps tight and handed the VIP a headset then slid into the flight engineer's station. "You ever took a ride in a Hellcat before, Mister Vasquez?"

"No," the CEO replied. He straightened his tie and cleared his throat. "I never had the privilege of serving in any capacity. My military experience has been as a contractor and consultant in the private sector."

"All secured back here, Cap," Brick reported.

"Copy that, Brick." Mongo adjusted the primary throttles and lifted up on the collective. The Hellcat shuddered as it lifted skyward and soared forward.

Pluto laughed. "Whew wee! You're in for one hell of a ride then. The run down Mullins Canyon on the eastern side of the Barris Mountains is one hairy ass ride. I hope you're buckled in good and tight. Mongo here is our craziest pilot."

"And the best pilot this side of the galactic core," Doc added.

"I don't know about all of that," Mongo said. "I think we're just going to take a nice steady ride back to base camp."

"A tour of the Canyon sounds quite invigorating, Captain," Vasquez said with a challenging tone.

Mongo turned in his seat, glancing back at the CEO.

Vasquez frowned. "Is that a problem?"

Mongo looked to Doc, then back to Vasquez, and smiled. "Not really, sir."

Doc let out a laugh, then turned to monitor the readouts at the engineer's station then keyed the intercoms. "Buckle up ladies. Time to thread the Devil's Eye."

Vasquez tugged on his restraints and adjusted his headset. "What's the Devil's Eye?"

Mongo made several adjustments to the controls then adjusted his own straps. "You'll see in about ninety seconds, sir."

The Hellcat lurched forward, slamming each of them back into their seats.

"You should be able to see the canyon coming up through the lower viewport," Mongo said over his shoulder to Vasquez.

"Yes," he replied, craning his neck to see from the rear jump seat.

Doc grunted a laugh. "Just sit back; it's about to get a whole lot closer."

"Ready, willing, and able!" Mongo shouted followed by a unanimous *Oorah* from the rest of the crew.

The Hellcat banked hard to the right before inverting. He nosed the gunship over, diving straight for the canyon floor, rotating one hundred and eighty degrees before pulling up hard and rolling sideways to slip through the canyon opening.

Vasquez let out an excited yelp as the massive Hellcat transport rolled, pulled hard right, hard left, nosed up, inverted, and rolled into a wider section of the canyon where they cruised along smoothly.

"Where did you learn to fly like this, Captain?" Vasquez asked.

Mongo snorted. "Nowhere really. Just flight school and lots of practice."

"Don't let the kid fool ya," Pluto said, interrupting the conversation. "He's a natural is what he is. And if you think this is something, you should see what he can do in a Fulcrum."

"A Fulcrum?"

"Yeah," Doc began. "The Fairchild Republic FR-AX Fulminus II. It's the primary gunship that the 5th Brigade uses besides the Hellcats."

"What's so different about them?" Vasquez asked.

"Fulcrums are a much smaller craft compared to these Hellcat heavy gunships," Mongo said. "They are one of the most heavily relied upon pieces of equipment by most fighting forces."

Doc laughed. "Yeah, 'cause they're damned effective, and you can't beat their maneuverability."

"Reliable and easy to maintain, too," Pluto added.

"With Vertical Take-Off and Landing capability built around their tried and true armor shredding twin 20mm Gauss cannons and Executor multi-barrel laser cannon mounted in its nose," Mongo continued, "you can't get much more deadly. They aren't the fastest of the fighter craft still available, but they are nimble and tough as nails with four independent engine nacelles mounted to the quad wing design. Heavily armored and armed, with sixteen hardpoint weapons mounts across the wings and lower fuselage. They are a force to be reckoned with in any firefight."

"I'd say so," Vasquez said. "They sound more than impressive."

"I'm sure that we could set up a demonstration while you're here."

"That would be wonderful."

A short time later, the Hellcat settled into her designated parking spot on the flightline of the Delz-Tik Industries Expeditionary Base Camp.

"Doors opening," Pluto announced as he donned his mask.

"Copy that, Pluto," Mongo acknowledged. "Primaries coming down, switching to APU power."

"Brick, you've got the post-flight inspection." Mongo unstrapped his harness and climbed out of the pilot's seat. "I'll escort you to the command center aboard the Delz-Tik dropship whenever you're ready, Mister Vasquez."

"That's kind of you, Captain." Vasquez released his harness and straightened his suit. "But I'd prefer to see the dig site first."

"I can do that as well, sir."

"And can we drop the 'sir'?" Vasquez asked. "It seems too formal and stuffy. Dorian will suffice."

"Yes, si… I'll try my best."

"Good. That's all we can hope for, isn't it?"

Mongo nodded in agreement.

"And what do I call you, Captain?"

"The callsign is Mongo."

Vasquez smiled. "Mongo it is."

Mongo led the way off of the flightline toward the dig site. Workers bustled about the crumbled remains of the Old Empire bunker entrance set into the rocky mountainside. They moved loaders of earth from the fabricated tunnel as the pair approached.

"What exactly are you hoping to find here?" Mongo asked.

"We're not sure exactly. But any Old Empire technology, especially a bio lab, will be well worth the effort."

"With everything we saw during the Succession Wars, I'd think bioweapons would be the last thing we'd want to turn loose."

"Rest assured, any specimens will be destroyed, but the research alone would be worth its weight in gold. Think of the pharmaceutical applications if a new delivery method or activator were discovered."

"And you'd be able to corner the market on the application."

Vasquez pointed a gun finger at Mongo. "Exactly."

"But what if there isn't anything down there?"

"Then we take a loss." Vasquez shrugged. "That's all part of the gamble."

The pair made their way into the constructed tunnel and, taking an unattended cart, quickly made their way to the end. Drill crews worked at multiple points around the face of a heavy vault door.

"Notification was sent once the team finally uncovered the complex's entrance," Vasquez continued. "I wanted to be here for the opening."

"Mister Vasquez," a worker in dirty yellow coveralls shouted over the noise of drilling as he approached. "I didn't know that you'd arrived." The man held out his hand in greeting to the CEO. "Gary Pletz, Project lead."

"Only just, Mister Pletz," Vasquez said as he took the man's hand and shook. "What's our status?"

"We are over ninety percent through the door's locking mechanism," Pletz boasted. "We could break through at any moment, honestly. We would have gotten through faster, but the locking rod material is some kind of alloy that none of my team has ever encountered before. The only thing that will even mar its surface has been a sub-sonic drilling rig."

The sound of wailing sirens suddenly filled the tunnel from the base camp outside.

"What is that?" Vasquez asked.

"That's the threat warning," Mongo said. "We've got something inbound. Stay here. You'll be safe inside the mountain," he said as he hurried back out of the tunnel. Mongo ran as fast as his legs would move across the dusty sands. Pluto and Brick were detaching the refueling line to their Hellcat as Mongo rounded the corner of the Delz-Tik dropship.

"What the hell's going on?"

"Thought you'd tell us," Pluto said, then pulled his mask to the side and spit.

A low rumble filled the air. Mongo searched the skies for the threat. Out of the east, three contrails low to the ground headed for their position.

Mongo jumped on board and slid into the pilot's seat. "Get her buttoned up. We gotta go! NOW!" Without waiting for an all-clear, he activated the primaries and started the launch sequence. "Where's Doc?"

"He decided he didn't want to wait on your slow ass," Pluto said as he strapped himself into the gunner's harness. "Said something about you'd rather brown nose and kiss that CEO's ass than do your actual job."

"Oh, ha ha ha," Mongo said sarcastically. "It's called customer relations."

"No, it's called sucking up to the man." Pluto laughed.

"So where's Doc?"

"He jumped into his Fulcrum and scrambled with Alpha squad just as soon as the sirens went off."

Defensive countermeasures ignited across the surface of the spherical Delz-Tik dropship. Tracer rounds streaked out across the sky in the direction of the inbound bogies.

Mongo pushed the primary throttles to the stops and pulled up on the control collective. The Hellcat gunship leapt into the sky as the first cruise missile exploded, detonated by the curtain of lead fired by the dropship's point defense guns. The next three missiles impacted the parking ramp. Three of Delta Squad's rhinos took the brunt of the first missile. Two of Charlie Squad's Hellcats were no better than scrap while half of Bravo Squad lay scattered across the sandy desert.

"Holy, shit," Mongo said quietly into his mic.

"Bravo Squad just got fucked!" Brick shouted.

"I know Bear Claw, Bender, and Can-Do were all in their birds getting ready to launch," Pluto said in a solemn tone.

Mongo keyed his transmitter. "DTI Control, this is Right-Hand. Give me some direction. Someone needs to get fucked for that."

"Right-Hand, be advised. Three fast movers inbound, bearing 023 from your position, trained on base camp. Their profiles suggest a flight of Reavers. Scout drones are also picking up several ground contacts heading this way from 010. Transmitting threat data, now."

Doc let out a worried breath. "Seriously? Reavers?"

"What's wrong, Doc? You scared or something?" Mongo nosed the Hellcat due north and gunned the throttles. "How many other ships do we have, Command?"

"Doc's alive!" Brick shouted.

"Of course I'm still alive, FNG."

"Ground crews are doing what they can at the moment," Command reported. "We have your Hellcat and three Fulcrums airborne. You have forward command, Right-Hand."

"You two get ready back there," Mongo said over his shoulder then keyed the transmitter. "Copy that Command. We're on it. Right-Hand has field control. Doc, who's with you?"

"Casper and JAR," Doc replied.

"Can you handle those Reavers while we check out the ground units?"

"Are you kidding?" Casper said, breaking into the transmission. "We can take out those fixed-wing bastards with our hands tied behind our backs."

"Alright then!" Mongo laughed. "If the hand of God isn't enough…"

"…You call the Fist!" The comm channel erupted in unanimous chants.

In minutes, combat chatter swamped the comms as Doc's flight of Fulcrums engaged the enemy fighter-bombers.

"Dammit, JAR!" Doc shouted over the comms. "Casper! Do you have eyes on JAR? Did he punch out?"

"Negative," Casper grunted over the comm channel. His breathing sounded like he'd replied in the middle of a high-G turn.

"Bastards got JAR," Brick said in a shaken tone.

"We don't know that yet," Mongo replied. "He might have made it the same as Rabbit made it. Now get your head back in the game, ground targets ahead." Mongo keyed the transmitter. "Command, this is Right-Hand. I have visual on ground targets. Please advise."

"Copy that Right-Hand. Engage at will."

"Lock and load, kid," Pluto cheered.

Mongo transmitted across all frequencies. "Unknown convoy, turn around immediately or you will be fired upon. This is your only warning."

Flashes of tracer fire suddenly lit up the sky. Mongo banked the Hellcat left, steering clear of the enemy rounds.

Pluto laughed. "You expected anything less from them?"

"Not really." Mongo nosed the Hellcat skyward, gaining altitude as he swung the gunship wide. "Pluto, can you make out anything on that convoy?"

"Hang on, Cap." Pluto detached from his gunner's harness at the side door and slid into the flight engineer's seat at the rear of the cockpit.

"Looks like a half dozen APC's, a few hover-transports, and…Whoa."

"Whoa? That doesn't sound good."

"No, it's not. There are two Labaqui main battle tanks in the middle."

"We can't let those tanks get within range of base camp or they'll obliterate it." Mongo keyed the comms. "Left-Hand, this is Right-Hand. Doc, we could use a bit of extra firepower over here. They've got two Labaqui bearing down on base camp along with a slew of APC's."

Grunted breathing replied over the comms. "You're on…your own. Kind of…busy."

"Shit."

"I'll second that," Pluto said.

Brick cleared his throat. "What's so special about those tanks?"

"The APCs and transports won't be a problem in the slightest, but with our current loadout, we'd have to be in perfect alignment to really do any damage to those two Labaqui. They are heavily armored with kinetic shielding on top of it."

"Shit, boy," Pluto said with a snorted chuckle. "Anything that one of those tanks hits with its 303 caliber main gun tends to not exist anymore. It just goes poof and becomes one with the universe and shit."

"You have such a wonderful way with words, you know that, Pluto?" Mongo let out a laughing sigh. "I've got an idea." He guided the Hellcat due north away from the convoy. "Launch the scout drones."

"Wait? What? Why would we launch the scout drones? The small pulse lasers on those things won't even touch the armor on those APCs."

"We don't need them to," Mongo said. "We just need them to be a pain in the ass distraction while I bring us back around for a strafing run. Maybe I can take out a few of those APCs on the first pass."

"That we can manage," Pluto said. "Brick, fire up the drone station. You take the primary two and I'll drive the secondary units from up here."

"On it, Sarge," Brick replied.

"Bring them in as low as you can," Mongo ordered. "Hopefully, the convoy doesn't spot them until they are swarming on top of them."

Mongo veered the Hellcat wide as the scout drones launched, soaring across the sandy terrain only a few meters off the deck. The two pairs of flying disk scout drones zipped between the vehicles in the convoy, firing at exposed equipment or exposed viewports. Their small pulse lasers were about as effective against the armored vehicles as a laser pointer was to a cat.

Mongo turned the Hellcat in line with the rear of the convoy, keeping his altitude as close to the deck as possible. "Keep it up. Coming in hot for an attack run. See if you can't take out a few of their smaller guns. Maybe melt the barrels or something."

Mongo glanced back over his shoulder and could see Pluto targeting the driver of one of the transport trucks. "You're sure asking a lot, you know that, Cap? These things don't have much kick to them at all. They were designed to be used for crowd control more than anything."

"Well, just keep being the annoying asshole that you are so maybe they don't notice us creeping up their tailpipe."

As if on cue, small arms fire from the rearmost transport peppered the nose of the gunship. Keeping the nose of the Hellcat low, Mongo adjusted the altitude above the convoy. The twin wingtip-mounted Gauss cannons and the belly-mounted heavy Gatling laser rained hell down onto the rearmost transport. Mongo selected the two APCs just ahead of the transport on his tactical display and flipped up a bright red button guard on the control yoke.

"Wolverines away!"

"Wolverines!" Pluto and Brick shouted in unanimous reply.

Four of the small anti-material missiles soared out from their underwing pylons and exploded moments after. The explosion propelled the eight, twelve-inch long Armor Piercing flechette rounds through the armor plating of the APCs. This allowed their secondary High Explosive charges to do the maximum amount of damage possible to the enemy vehicles from the inside. Mongo pulled the triggers on the control yoke, strafing the remainder of the convoy before banking hard and peeling away. The two rearmost APCs hit by the Wolverine missiles smoked as the HE charges did their job, setting fire to everything inside the vehicles.

Target lock alarms erupted, and the tactical display flashed red, pinpointing the forward battle tank.

"Hang on back there. Things are about to get bumpy."

Mongo activated the Hellcat's countermeasures and rolled hard to port, pulling up and away from the convoy.

"Right-Hand, this is the Left," Doc came over the comms. "Casper is down, and I've got my hands full with two of these assholes. The third fast mover is inbound on your position.

"Great. Just what we needed," Pluto said with a laugh. "Tell him to bring the rest of the party while he's at it."

"Shut it, Pluto!" Mongo pointed the Hellcat's nose skyward then arced back and cut the throttles, letting the gunship freefall backward.

"Oh, God! We're going to die!" Brick screamed.

The Hellcat began to rotate as it plummeted groundward. Two missiles streaked past the gunship, harmlessly arcing off into the desert sands.

"That's it," Mongo shouted. "Missiles off course. Hang on!" He re-engaged the main engines, pushed the main throttles to full, and pulled back on the control yoke. The gunship rocked hard and slid sickeningly sideways as it fell out of the sky.

"Oh, God, oh, God, oh, God," Brick cried.

"Pull it together shit stain!"

"Will both of you shut up!" Mongo fought against the controls. "I'm trying to save our collective asses up here!" He adjusted the maneuvering thrusters to stabilize their fall then pulled hard on the control yoke. Target lock alarms resounded once again.

"Can either of you do something useful like, oh, I don't know, maybe target that launcher!"

"Already on it, Cap," Pluto replied.

Mongo rolled the Hellcat right, banked, dispensed countermeasures, and banked hard left. Another nearby explosion rocked the gunship.

"Sooner would be better than later!"

Mongo nosed the Hellcat toward the ground, changing course to make another pass at the convoy. "Let's see if that tank crew likes a missile up their own asses." Feet from the dusty ground, he guided the Hellcat on target and let loose all guns. He slid the gunship sideways to keep his nose on target. The cannons turned what remained of the APCs and transports into little more than scrap metal.

"Watch it, Cap," Pluto shouted. "That missile mount is turning in our direction.

"Well then do something about it."

"I am, but this piddly laser is barely scorching the thing."

"Ram it with the drone or something." Mongo adjusted course to slide starboard, targeting the main battle tanks on his tactical display with the few remaining shredder missiles. "Wolverines away," he called out. He continued to lay down Gauss and laser burst fire, disabling the remaining APCs as the missiles impacted the two Labaqui main battle tanks.

"Oh, what the hell, Mongo?" Pluto shouted. "You just killed my drones."

"And those missile racks to boot, so quit your bitching."

A loud beep sounded from the control console followed by, "*Ammunition level low.*"

"Should we pull out the Barts, Cap?" Brick asked.

Pluto laughed. "You're kidding, right, kid? The 12.7mm Bart rounds won't do nothing against a main battle tank except scratch the paint and piss it off."

Radar warnings sounded from the main console.

"We're being painted!" Pluto shouted over the alarms.

Mongo chuckled as he nosed the gunship forward and in the direction of the radar contact. "Oh, no shit, Sherlock. I think the alarms might have given that away."

"Just trying to be helpful, Cap."

"Hang on and shut it!" Mongo adjusted their course, skimming just above the moon's dusty surface at maximum speed. Two smoky white trails streaked across the yellow-tinted sky high above.

"Shit! Bogie at twenty thousand feet, Cap. That isn't going to make things easy."

Mongo banked hard left, staying as close to the ground as possible.

"I see him. Gotta shake those missiles before we can deal with him."

The ground exploded in a shower of dust and rock just ahead of the gunship. Mongo rolled right and pulled back on the yoke. "Holy shit!"

"At least we can deal with the Reaper," Pluto said. "But those Labaqui are going to vaporize us if we stay still for too long. Come about to three zero one."

"Copy that, coming around to three zero one."

"Maybe we can shake him around those mountains and get out of range of those tanks." Pluto cycled through the missile jamming frequencies. "Looks like they are running an old Takan frequency on those missiles. I can at least keep those off our backs for now. Pass off control of the laser turret to me so you can concentrate on flying this heap."

"Copy that. Turret control is yours, Sarge. What's the Reaver's altitude?"

"He's still hanging out on high. Looks like he's turning to come around for another pass."

"There's no way we can outrun a Reaver."

"And he'll pick us off before we can get high enough to line up a clean shot at him."

The ground erupted again, coming up a bit short and ahead of them off their port side.

"Shit. Picking up six new contacts all inbound on our position."

"I thought you were jamming them."

"I am," Pluto shouted. "They must be laser-guided."

Mongo adjusted their course, banking hard to port. "Let's see if that weapons officer is good enough to paint a moving target pulling evasive maneuvers." He shifted course again while changing altitude randomly.

The ground nearby exploded in a shower of rocky debris.

"Can you get us out of range of those tanks?" Pluto shouted.

"I'm working on it." Mongo laughed. "Maybe we should have just stayed in place by the tanks and let the Reaver blow them up for us."

"That has got to be the most ballsy, hold my beer thought to ever come out of your mouth, Cap. Okay, I'm game."

"Wait," Brick broke in. "We're going to do what?"

"Land on a tank."

Brick whimpered and crossed himself. "Oh, God."

Pluto burst out in hysterical laughter. "You better pray, 'cause that might be the only way we make it out of this alive."

The two main battle tanks continued toward the Delz-Tik base camp, taking the occasional shots at the gunship as Mongo zig-zagged his way around to their position. He brought the Hellcat to a sudden stop behind the aim of the main turrets, hovering and strafing sideways to keep out of their direct line of fire.

"Cap," Pluto said. "Three birds still airborne and heading straight for us."

"ETA?"

"Twelve seconds."

"Taking back control of the laser."

"Copy that," Pluto replied.

Mongo aimed the Hellcat's Gatling laser turret at the treads of the lead tank and opened fire.

"Eight," Pluto called.

The turret of the lead tank continued to track in the direction of the gunship as Mongo maneuvered closer.

"Six."

Sliding left ever so slightly, Mongo rotated to the right to aim at the second battle tank and set the belly of the gunship down on the roof of the lead Labaqui then immediately touched back off.

"Four."

Mongo pushed the throttles to full power and banked away hard, circling away in the direction of the incoming missiles.

"Two."

Mongo let out a bestial roar.

Brick wrapped his arms around himself, continuing to pray.

The gunship bucked forward, nose aimed at the ground. Warning alarms sounded from across the console. The Hellcat lurched nose up at a sickening rate as Mongo fired emergency landing thrusters. The gunship bellied in, skidding to a slow stop as she slid along the dusty ground. She came to a stop facing the remains of the two main battle tanks.

Mongo let out a long sigh and coughed. "That didn't go as well as I'd hoped" He tapped at the dead console and cycled all switches to their startup position. "Sound off, meatheads!"

Brick chortled. "I'm alive, Cap."

"You owe me a beer," Pluto said with a groan. He tapped at the main engineering display then activated the Hellcat's APU's. "You should have emergency power, Cap."

Mongo flipped a series of switches on the main console, running through the emergency startup sequence. He lifted the finger lift on the throttles, but nothing happened. "I've got nothing up here, Pluto."

"Dammit. Hold your horses." Pluto unbuckled his harness and pulled an access panel from under the engineering console. "Shit, that's what I was afraid of."

"Freaking start-up relays were knocked out of their sockets."

Mongo looked back over his shoulder. "Can you fix it?"

"Yeah," the veteran mechanic said, scratching at his stubbled chin. "Hey, Brick. Grab me a few feet of that eight gauge wire from the supply compartment."

Mongo scanned the skies, searching for the enemy Reaver when a glint of light high to the south caught his eye. "You'd better hurry. Looks like our friend might be turning back for another run.

"Come on, Kid. Get the lead out and light a fire under your fucking ass!" Pluto pulled a flashlight and a pair of wire cutters from his breast pocket then biting down on the cutters, shimmied himself into the console. Light rattling sounds were immediately followed by the sound of something plastic being thrown against the far wall of the cockpit.

"What the hell are you doing?"

"Checking the relays. What the hell does it look like I'm doing?"

"Getting comfy for nap time."

"Oh, ha, ha. Brick!" Pluto shouted. "Where's that wire?"

Brick suddenly appeared at the cockpit entrance with a small roll of wire in hand. "Right here, Sergeant."

"Well don't stand there mouth breathing. Fucking hand it to me!"

Brick fumbled with the roll of wire and then handed it off to Pluto. "Oh, yeah. Sorry Sergeant."

"You'll be sorry. Fucking FNG." He stripped the insulation away from the end of the wire with his teeth then cut a few inches away from the roll before stripping the opposite end.

"And what exactly are you trying to accomplish now?"

"I'm bypassing the bullshit safety switches and hot wiring the injectors. She won't run anything like she had been, but she should at least fire up and run enough to get us out of here."

"How are we supposed to outrun a Reaver?"

Pluto chuckled. "Get out and push. Now start this bitch and get us out of here."

Mongo turned back in his seat and lifted the throttle finger lifts. The Hellcat's primary engines roared to life. Lights and warnings flashed across the main console as radar lock warnings blared through the otherwise silent compartment.

"Hang onto something, ladies!" Mongo pushed the throttles to full power and the gunship's airframe shuddered, lifting skyward once more.

"Buckle in, kid!" Pluto climbed into the engineer's seat just as the Hellcat banked hard right in an attempt to evade whatever was heading their way.

"I'm not ready!"

"Too late! Just hold onto something!"

Mongo glanced over his shoulder as Pluto brought up the radar. Two red blips sped toward their position followed by a third blip that was crossing from south to north. "Two birds inbound, Cap. I can't tell you if they are guided or targeting with radar."

"What's the status on the laser?"

Pluto laughed. "Offline. After that belly flop, we'd honestly be lucky if there's anything left to salvage."

Mongo cycled through the gunship's status screens. "Countermeasures are gone too. We're out of missiles and the Gauss cannons are out of ammo."

"We could throw the FNG at them," Pluto suggested.

"Funny! How about we don't," Brick added.

"Bob and weave, Cap. Bob and weave. Try to make it to that mountain range if you can."

"You say that like a pregnant whale is supposed to corner on a dime, Pluto."

"Shit! Impact in ten, Cap. Missiles just made a hard turn in our direction."

Mongo rolled the ship right and began a low G banking turn. The airframe shuddered and creaked under the strain.

"Hold together baby."

"Eight."

The Hellcat rolled left and once again shuddered as the G load strained the airframe.

"Six."

"I'm open to suggestions!"

The radar lock warnings suddenly ceased. Mongo looked back over his shoulder at the engineer's station. The two earlier blips were now missing from the display. "What the hell just happened?"

"I don't know," Pluto replied, "but we have a new contact closing fast from O eight three at eight hundred and thirty knots and six new birds airborne from the new contact."

"Shit!" Mongo adjusted the course once again.

"Right-Hand, this is Left-Hand. Hope you don't mind me taking a swing at this asshat."

Pluto let out a triumphant yell.

"By all means, Doc. Have at him."

"Good, cause this asshole is the one that took out JAR and Casper. I owe him one hell of an ass-whooping."

"We'd give you a hand, but we're barely airborne at the moment."

Mongo caught a flash of explosions high above toward the northwest. The fiery remains of the Reaver tumbled from the yellow-tinted sky.

"You good up there, Doc?"

"Yup. Just peachy. Let's head home."

Mongo adjusted his course and keyed the base camp frequency. "DTI Base Camp, this is Right-Hand. Mission accomplished. Heading home."

"Mongo," the colonel's voice boomed across the comms. "If any of you have any missiles left, get back here ASAP and shove them up these corporate fucks' ass!"

"What the hell?" Doc mumbled over the team frequency.

"Repeat DTI Base. Last transmission not clear."

"I said to blow that drop ship out of the fucking sky, Captain!"

On the edge of the horizon, Mongo could make out the spherical shape of the Delz-Tik dropship as it lifted off, heading for orbit.

"What in the hell is going on?" Pluto said with a slow gasp.

"Let's not get stupid, Captain," Dorian Vasquez said over the base camp frequency.

"Vasquez? What's going on? Why are you lifting off? The threat has been eliminated."

"And while you were off doing a bang-up job of protecting our assets, we discovered that the Old Empire facility was completely barren. Just a concrete hole in the ground. And I'm sure that you can appreciate running certain projects on a shoestring budget as it is. As the CEO of Delz-Tik Industries, I took it upon myself to cut our losses on this failed project and return home."

"But what about us? How are we supposed to get off this rock?"

"I suppose you'll have to hitch a lift with someone else," Vasquez said with a low chuckle. "I've heard that several transports are running out of Hub Town weekly."

"That son of a bitch," Pluto growled.

"Hey, Doc."

"Yeah, Mongo?"

"Got any missiles left?"

"Nah. I used the last of them on that Reaver."

Mongo let out a long sigh. "I was afraid you were going to say that."

Doc formed up along the port side of the Hellcat as they watched the corporate dropship continue skyward, unabated.

The End

The Flaming Bomb
By Sergio Palumbo

The graying, long-haired, seventy-five-year-old professor was concluding the lesson for his students. He had just posted instructions on the wide electronic whiteboard which connected directly to the neural shunts of the few young ones sitting at the desks, when two people approached the open door and stopped just before coming inside. As the aged man saw the two, he immediately knew that they were high-ranking officers of the Special Teams Units—and not the usual ones you could find inside the military school—even though he didn't imagine they had come for him. But it didn't take long before he was aware that something important was going on.

"Captain Robert Cordingly, your presence is requested at once. Please take leave of your students and follow us to meet our colonel." The tall white-skinned commandant told him what to do with a cold, straight-forward tone of voice, his short blond hair framing his almost square head. He seemed to wear his battalion shoulder badge—a circular drawing thinly outlined in gray with yellowish tinting—as a second skin: those insignia were rarely seen in the field or around, as a matter of fact. His massive black associate, a major with dark vivid eyes and the same greenish-blue uniform, gestured to the elderly captain indicating the direction to go, as if they didn't expect any resistance from him.

"What's the matter, sirs?" the professor found the courage to ask them. It was uncommon enough that his lessons were interrupted by a sudden visit like that, but it was even weirder that two high-ranking members of the Earth Space Army needed to talk to him. After all the interrogations, studies,

"

examinations, and medical treatments he had undergone when he was much younger, he thought that he had nothing else to fear when spotting officers of the Special Units like them, but he was obviously wrong.

The commandant frowned for a while, as if he was asking himself if it was the moment to explain anything to him, then he plainly spoke: "They're back."

Those words made Robert feel ill at ease. He still could sense that great fear deep inside his gut: the visceral reaction he had felt so long ago, caused by everything that those beings had brought for him and Mankind itself.

It was the middle of September and twenty-five-year-old Robert Cordingly's recon team was marching along the dirty path that the automated cutting devices—known as meadow-eaters—had opened for the soldiers so they could move freely through that portion of the gray undergrowth covering a vast portion of the reddish ground. They had been scouting the area since the early morning, and the warm temperatures hindered them in their search. The meadow-eaters were ruthless while doing their job. What was left afterwards was a muddy surface with only a few small leaves scattered here and there, which stained the team's reinforced footwear when they walked on them. Their priority wasn't to keep their uniforms clean, nor their skin or short hair, of course. They proceeded with only one goal: to accomplish their present duty.

The twenty well-armed military ships from their spectacular Fighter wing had reached the orbiting position in that sector of space two days ago. As soon as the time to start deploying the troops had come, they had been sent to the surface of the orange-colored planet—provisionally named Auxesia—which was twice the size of Earth. Because of its slow rotation, it had long-lasting seasons and acceptable atmospheric conditions for humans. That world now lay below their hull, along with the scout-crafts, some drop pods full of specialized teams, and armored sections meant to secure the ground of that alien place. The landmass was divided into ten small island continents. They were ready to attack at the drop of a hat, in case they were ordered to do so.

Their 562-1-T team was made up of nine men: the Sergeant, Brett, the slender Assistant Team Leader; the Space Radio Operator, Hoet; Alrek, the Point Man; Anete, the appointed sniper; Petruso, Danya, Heorhiy, and Robert Cordingly himself. The operational zone that day stretched the length of twenty miles, covering a wide area of terrain containing different small leafy trees standing no more than the height of a young boy. The land to its west appeared to be largely rolling shrubs once the southern hills in the distance were passed.

Just like every soldier assigned to the present task, Robert wore a wide dark metallic helmet endowed with operational pictures inside, the usual close-combat enhanced glasses, and the increased body armor in dark yellowish-gray, similar to the peculiar shades of the alien ground and vegetation that stretched all around. He had added defenses hidden and integrated into his uniform, along with the common load equipment, emergency power supply, a personal cooling system, and enough food and water to last a week.

The TLE energy-rifle with a short hand-guard and empowered round box magazines, was the very accurate main service weapon of every man in the Earth Space Army. There were all kinds of variant devices for it: like optical sights, and a twenty-inch barrel which was easily customizable with many add-ons. For instance, there was a folding bipod, removable handle, silencers, biotech machinery, bomb launchers, grappling ropes, etc. In free fall environments you had to use some completely different or upgraded versions of weaponry—each of them also carried a 12x12mm. pistol, a modern knife for hand-to-hand fighting, commonly named 'Last Farewell', and a small air burst weapon—usually an APL. But you could only kill wild beasts using that weapon, as it was never suggested to be used as your primary sidearm, unless you had nothing else to protect yourself and you were absolutely desperate…

Robert was twenty-five-years-old at that time, with a massive build and a nose that was a bit too small for the rest of his face that he was used to inadvertently scratching here and there during drills. Robert had always had an attentive mind and two feet that he had thought were too big. On the other hand, he didn't really mind as long as they took him wherever he wanted to go at a very fast pace.

The peculiar rose-colored skies of that world were not due to the nearest star's color, but mostly due to the reddish particles of the terrain, which came from the tiny flecks of dust staying up longer under such thin atmospheric conditions, along with the lack of wind. This gave the overall environment a sort of fairy-tale appearance. But they were having a relaxing trip now, and no fairy-like creatures were ever supposed to be found at the end of the road that lay in front of them—unless you included some monsters that frequently appeared in legends, which might actually come out sooner or later…After all, they knew so little about the planet that anything was possible.

As they marched, Robert increased his speed as he tried to reach Hoet and started whispering to him as soon as he caught up with his fellow soldier. Hoet was the most experienced soldier among them. He was the one appointed to connect to the active communications satellites deployed around the planet of Auxesia before the drop had started.

Hoet was always in touch with the personnel from the aerial port that had been positioned in the northern continent to support the entire operation. The team had to go through him if they needed an aeromedical evacuation, and even their Commander had to wait for his authorization—just in case…

"No news from the other attack battalions yet? Are they in position now?" Robert asked.

"They are ready," Hoet replied, his characteristically low voice sounding like a continuous scratch on a rock, both azure irises looking lost. "They're just waiting for us to find the enemy."

"Well, we haven't seen any traces of them so far. It's not as if we can tell people that we found the enemy only to make them happy, you know…"

Hoet slowly turned his head and stared at him, stating in a plain way, "Funny, but not smart. Our automated identification technology is not something we can rely on under such uncertain circumstances. The aliens could interfere in ways still unknown to us. Our recon troops need us to confirm targets before reaching the exact operational area." After he finished speaking, he went back to listening to the information and data that filled the communication lines only he could effectively access.

"Uhm, you're right, indeed," Robert said, making a face, but his fellow soldier wasn't paying attention to him anymore. Trying to talk to Hoet was usually a waste of time, Robert told himself, as he had bad manners that always made you think you were wrong in the end.

Things went on as calmly as before for several more hours under that strangely colored vault of the heavens. Then something happened.

About time, Robert told himself. Hoet stopped walking and immediately turned to the rest of the recon team, simply uttering, "Our satellites spotted something. The order has been given. All men, prepare to reach that high point at the end of this plain, weapon in hand!"

He remembered he had thought at the time: *Without any support vehicles around?* But those were the orders, and there was nothing else to do—even though they were being sent to open ground with no hint of what they might find once they got up there. When he was much younger, Robert had never gone straight to school in the morning but had always taken the longest route possible. Of course, he wasn't in a hurry to get there and remain within those walls for most of the day, since he didn't like that place even though he knew he had to go. So, why were they taking the fastest route to the location of—possibly—an oncoming battle now? Wasn't that the most predictable course to take? Weren't the aliens themselves going to try to ambush them as soon as possible?

Those troublesome thoughts had a grip on Robert's mind at that time, but he knew he wasn't a high-ranking officer, so decisions about the deployment of troops and the overall strategy on the surface of Auxesia wasn't something that was up to him. He was a simple soldier at that time, even though he was sure he wasn't going to remain so for long.

As a matter of fact, Robert had always enjoyed fighting, and using his hands to beat someone—he was better at it than studying, which was exactly why he had enlisted three years earlier. It had been right on time for the first contact with the new alien species called Hulowrs and for the following troubles that had occurred soon thereafter. It seemed things would probably lead up to a war if one of the two opposing sides didn't stop demanding that they be given sole ownership of that space sector and all the planets within it. This was because that zone looked very promising, being very rich in resources.

It was exactly for that purpose that the Earth Space Army and their Fighter wing of spaceships had been sent there in a hurry, in order to secure Auxesia. Troopers like him had been dropped to the surface, ready to face any trouble or battle mechanism the aliens might be making use of on the ground to force them to withdraw. Likely coming from a high-gravity planet that hadn't been heard of yet, the Hulowrs were short and broad-shoulder beings, with long unruly hair, greenish leathery skin, and a prominent mouth—or so the only report they had about the species indicated, which was not much. Not that their appearance would change anything, anyway. *But were the humans really ready to fight a war with these aliens?* They knew very little about these newcomers who had only recently reached this point in space—so wasn't it a dangerous move and might it bring some unexpected consequences?

All that made sense to Robert was that he was finally going to put into practice the months of training he had undergone when he had entered the Space Army. He looked forward to shooting off many high-powered shells against Earth's opponents, finally being able to operate the costly and highly-engineered outfit and equipment he was endowed with. An opportunity like this didn't happen frequently on Earth or on the few colonies Mankind had settled here and there so far, given the peaceful conditions they had been living under for so many years. But they had to be prepared and well experienced when they came into a situation like this.

By the end of the day Robert would be thinking of how wrong he was, and how undoubtedly innocent he still was at the time. However, his lack of understanding wouldn't make it any easier to forgive his superiors for the mistake they were going to make. Not that anyone could have expected what was going to happen next...

A small CCTV camera watched the professor hurriedly enter the room that he had been ordered to go into that morning, as soon as the doors opened. His chestnut eyes, the same color as his hair had once been, were subdued, but his senses were always ready to respond to anything that might happen.

This was a residual gift from the intensive training that he had undergone for years, when he was still in full military service. Much to his surprise, the superintendent he knew well—a dark-haired man who did perfectly run that school—wasn't sitting at the main desk. Instead, a man with a receding gray hairline was in his chair. There was no reason to point it out for now. *Better to wait*, he considered.

The short, middle-aged, high-ranking officer seemed not to be particularly interested in common formalities, apparently, as the briefing began almost immediately as soon as he introduced himself. "I'm Colonel Frank Voewt, Captain Cordingly. Please, have a seat."

Robert did as ordered and he heard the doors soundly closing behind him, both the blond-haired commandant of the Special Teams along with the black major stepping outside, leaving the two alone. The greenish walls all around seemed to almost completely wrap him in, while he focused on the gold, black, and orange rug that looked like an old print from afar but was really a series of strange concentric circles stretching to the desk before him.

"I temporarily borrowed this room from your present superintendent, as you can see." The tone of the man was plain and direct. The lines in his face made him appear chiseled and wise. "Do you like your job here, Captain? Do you miss the time when you still operated in active service?"

"Actually, it was long ago, sir, about fifty years. I've become a good teacher since then, or so I'd like to think," replied Robert.

"Teaching the most promising young boys and girls that will become our future soldiers is a great accomplishment, indeed. And your records tell me that you work very well."

"Thank you, sir. I'm glad you think so," the aged man nodded.

Some moments of silence followed as the colonel read some documents. Then he raised his azure eyes and looked at him. "Our headquarters received a message from outer space two days ago, and our Communication Section took its time before deciding what to do. We have been contacted again by the aliens known as Hulowrs."

Contacted? the professor thought, incapable of believing what he was hearing. *The only reason they might be contacting humans is to order them to surrender…what other request could have been sent?* Well, they had not come around or entered Earth Space Boundary yet, or else he would have known it, and in the worst way possible.

The cold eyes of the colonel were still staring at him, apparently waiting for a sort of reaction. Robert knew he had to say something and letting his eyes absentmindedly roam across the rug below didn't help him.

"I don't understand, sir. After all these years, why should they contact us?" he finally asked the superior who sat at the other end of the wooden desk full of many tablets and other electronic devices. Actually, a larger question that stood out in his mind was: *Why didn't the aliens destroy us all yet?*

"That is why I wanted to speak to you, Captain Cordingly."

"So, how may I be of help?" Robert asked. In his troubled mind, he was thinking: *After all I already did in the past…*

"Would you please briefly tell me what you experienced when you first met them about fifty years ago? A short recount of your operational deployment at that time would suffice," Voewt said.

Again? Robert sighed, lowering his eyes. It seemed that there was no way to get away from all of it, despite the long time that had gone by. "Of course, sir. I'll try to be more precise than I was before, even though many years have passed—I still have a clear recollection of what happened."

"I counted on it, Captain. I would expect nothing else from one of the brave soldiers of our Space Army dropped to Auxesia on that sad day."

Robert sighed again, his hands started moving slightly, nervously. Those were experiences that he still had nightmares about. So, he let himself remember it all, one more time…

Their stride had cut through the shrubs, and they had easily moved forward. As Danya, the first one of their scout team, reached the point where they could have a clear view of the area below indicated as the target, nothing seemed to be around. The young man sighed as he slowly shouldered his weapon, his dark eyes scanning the distance for any sign of their elusive target. Next to him, Robert was beginning to believe the enemy wasn't even present on the planet's surface. Having been out in the valleys below for about ten hours without sighting anything except local wildlife and some strangely shaped rocks hadn't cheered them up, of course, nor had it made things easier. What was really happening on that world today? Weren't they supposed to be meeting their adversaries soon, or at least their battle robots? Hadn't they all been sent there in order to stop the aliens from taking that place for themselves? So, where were they? And why did it seem like nothing was going to happen during the rest of the day? Questions without answers, time spent with no results…

The soldier squinted and calmed his breathing, slowly examining every shadow, shrub and rock around, looking for whatever unexpected—or dangerous— situation would present itself next, but he saw, one more time, nothing unusual. *There was nothing at all!* The only sounds that filled the area were the faint cries—or so they seemed—that a few local flying creatures, hidden in the gray undergrowth emitted from time to time, along with the gurgling of a small stream running in front of them.

Then, the small, polished surface of a reddish alien hull appeared in the distance, not far from a boulder. Such a structure seemed to provide some valuable protection against any direct hits, but there were no guns on the outside nor other defensive systems or entry points on its large sides. It was as if that Hulowr vehicle had always been there, but they hadn't been able to see it. *Was it some sort of cloaking device, or maybe a peculiar paint that made it move and land unseen?* The alien spacecraft appeared in full sight now, and that was just good enough.

But they couldn't expect what was next. They could have never imagined…

"What happened next?" It was the piercing low voice of the graying colonel that brought Robert back to his senses, removing that oppressive feeling he was experiencing during his story.

The Captain started speaking again, turning his eyes to the desk. "We were ready to go on, and I was included in the first group chosen to approach the unknown Hulowr vehicle and have a better look from a closer position. My heart beat wildly, and it was partly due to the agitation of the moment, but also to my inquisitiveness, because I really wanted to know how such a craft looked inside, the same as all the rest of the team who was down there. But there wasn't any movement from the alien crew, and we didn't hear anything moving inside. Everything seemed quiet, calm, and terribly silent in my opinion, but what other option did we have than to keep walking forward, waiting for it to do something?"

"So, you kept walking along until you arrived at the feet of the landing gears of the spacecraft, didn't you?"

"Yes, we did, even though the lack of sounds and movement made us feel uncertain and cautious, clearly…" Robert pointed out.

"What did you find when you got to the hull?"

"We stood up together, surrounding it—as we had been trained to do—with our energy-rifles in our hands and our fingers ready to activate maximum fire, in case it would be necessary to repel any assault or stop any enemies who might suddenly jump out at us from some hidden opening along that alien surface. But we never accomplished our last approach, as we all noticed a strange sizzle on the upper part of the craft. It was just a matter of seconds…there was no time to react. And then, we saw it…The Flaming Bomb! It appeared before our eyes like an expanding, towering burst that was rising to the sky, higher and higher, violently incinerating everything in its path and wiping out even the rocks themselves. All of us were caught unaware, and then its devastating effects began affecting all the men in my team."

"The fact is that there was no Flaming Bomb at all," the colonel made clear, making a disgusted face. That was something which had become pretty obvious over the course of the months subsequent to that unlucky expedition, and it was repulsive to recall such events, especially with someone who wasn't present on the battlefield of that distant alien world.

"True, sir. Actually, no one among us knew it at that time—not even our superiors in our orbiting spaceships—what was going on down there, on the surface of Auxesia…" the captain continued, his eyes lowering another time to the colorful rug on the floor.

Voewt nodded, then put his hands on the desk and appeared thoughtful. "What was ascertained afterwards was that a single Hulowr spacecraft had landed in the middle of the operational area you were ordered to scout. It had come unseen, and it was only by chance that our instrumentation had spotted it in the end. Or maybe only we were allowed to see it on purpose, at a certain moment, according to the will of those impenetrable aliens. In a way, all of you, the soldiers who were on the ground and all of our men aboard the military spaceships, saw that bomb exploding, and were seriously affected by the consequences of its activation."

Robert didn't look back at the colonel directly, because the recollections of that day were still deeply engraved in his mind.

"Even today, fifty years later, we still don't know how the Hulowrs made it, but they did, anyway. All of you were inadvertently exposed to some unknown weapon that forcibly entered your brain, enveloping your thoughts and overpowering you. All the soldiers felt their skin burning, their eyes becoming ash and the body being wrapped into a damn fire that was consuming their tissues, extremities, clothes, and equipment, all at the same time. And the same thing happened to all the military teams working on the planet, on all the ten continents of Auxesia. Not even our personnel in space could escape it."

"But it was just a sensation! Or, at least, that is what was discovered afterwards, according to explanations given by our scientists," Robert added, in an angry tone.

"Yes, it was, Captain Cordingly. That is what we discovered over the course of the time, but it wasn't certain nor plausible at that moment. Do you remember what happened next? What is your first memory when you were found on the ground?"

"When the drop pods of medical units finally reached Auxesia about twelve hours later, the alien spacecraft had already left the surface of the planet. The supporting frigates left in the rearguard were one light year away and presumed that no more danger was to be expected on the planet. Actually, their commanders didn't know if the ground was clear or not, but they also thought that if they wanted to search for any surviving soldiers, it was now or never."

"Please, go on…" Voewt insisted on that point.

"When I awoke, I immediately felt lost, confused, incapable of walking for some time and totally dejected. The same can be said about all the others who were in my team. *And that fear!* Inside our minds we all sensed the remains of that unstoppable pain we had felt all over our bodies. We looked down at our feet and at our hands just to be sure they were still there, as we could still clearly remember being burnt into ashes in a matter of seconds."

"However," the colonel added, staring at him, "in reality, it was reported finally that none of you were really wounded. Once all of the soldiers sent to that world were found unconscious and without any will left to fight combat, our headquarters decided it was better to take all the Space Army back and retreat to a safer zone nearer the farthest colonies Earth had already settled outside the External Boundary. As a matter of fact, whatever the unknown weapon was that the enemies had used, it had also affected the crewmembers on all of our vessels orbiting that planet. Only the emergency automated systems onboard had prevented their hulls from crashing into satellites or the other ships nearby, which might have caused a great disaster."

"So, we were spared, but for what purpose? What is the strategy behind it all?" Robert dared ask the colonel, who sat with a distinct frown on his face. It was of no importance at all that fire had not spread over his body during the activation of the Flaming Bomb, and that it was only a figment of their imaginations, as he couldn't prevent himself from believing that it all was true and that he was dying at that time. He remembered that since that moment, after the long and painful months he had undergone in order to try to find a healing treatment—help that was never received—he had even tried to resign. However, General Headquarters back on the Moon had asked him to stay and work alongside the superior officers as a counselor or a teacher experienced at war who could still prove to be useful for the Earthlings' cause, as a matter of fact.

"Their strategy is still unclear. What is certain, however, is that the Hulowrs on Auxesia didn't kill you all that day, and that they did not even try to invade our nearest outposts in space afterwards. They had made it so that we all understood that they didn't want us to be in that sector anymore, and what had happened appeared to be merely a serious warning, something we had never experienced before. As you also know, those facts deeply changed our overall strategy, as Earth's military didn't dare to enter the space ruled by those powerful aliens again and it also forced us to head for other areas instead of that one in order to provide new colonies for the immigrants coming from our home planet who wanted to start a new life away from here. This is a policy we have followed until today."

"But the question still remains…why did they act that way? And how?" Robert insisted, his hands still moving nervously.

"The how still is uncertain, but we have discovered that what those aliens instilled deeply inside your minds was meant to keep you at a distance, and not only from their area of supremacy or their persons themselves, but also from any craft, structure, or mechanisms built by them, or that contained some specific metals or minerals the Hulowrs used. Do you know of a better way to make you leave and stay away so as not to suffer the same consequences again? Who would ever accept to undergo the unbearable effects of that Flaming Bomb on their body and mind, even if they knew it was not real? Who might accept to die in such a monstrous way another time, even if such a passing wasn't real? And moreover, how could anyone force his thoughts not to take that weapon as a true threat, a bloody attack that can't be stopped and that can destroy your skin, your brain, and everything that makes you a living man? Not even one of our psychic officers—and there were a few who happened to be very powerful and experienced that day in the operational area—proved capable of resisting or opposing such unbelievable strength, nor sensed it on time to warn the others around," the colonel explained in his plain voice.

"So, there is no reason why they should have left our troops alive on the ground by then," asked the professor. "Why didn't they simply conquer all of us? Who could have stopped them? Definitely not the Fighter wing of our expeditionary force…" he inquired.

"For a very long time, we didn't discover any answer, this much is true. We thought that they only wanted to keep us away from the worlds they asserted to be theirs, like Auxesia, and from those valuable resources. Or we thought that, maybe, we just didn't deserve their full interest at that time, as our planet was of no strategic importance to them. We had clearly been beaten hard, completely defeated, and they might have done exactly what they wanted against our unconscious army that sad day…though, they didn't! Undoubtedly, the fact that our men had been stopped so easily, by means of a weapon that had been launched from a single small spacecraft made all of our efforts and cautious deployment of soldiers on the ground appear laughable."

"Indeed, sir." Robert nodded.

"When our soldiers were sure that such a powerful alien instrument of war was connected to something that was hidden in the structure of all of their ships, buildings, and even pieces of scrap metal built by the Hulowrs and left somewhere in space—and that any closeness to such objects would activate the technologically-provoked mental illness—we were aware that we had no other choice: retreat, move away from those overwhelming adversaries and hope that they would never enter and assault our space. What could our armies do if their vessels ever approached our farthest colonies, one day or another? And what if they decided to invade Earth? Would we be able to leave our home planet forever and start a long search for a new place to live, somewhere, always retreating? And then, how long would we be safe…? I can't even imagine a continuous escape which would drive us all further and further away from our homes. Maybe it's just because I'm a military officer and I prefer to fight, but I think you can easily understand my point of view. But there is no way to oppose such mind-blowing enemies if they decided they wanted to come here. There is no means of winning a single battle against them, you know."

"So, what's the matter with the Hulowrs now? Why did they contact us again after Auxesia?" Robert appeared to be very doubtful, and he didn't think anyone would ever answer his questions. But he was wrong.

The officer drew a breath before he began talking again, slowly and deliberately. "As I said before, for a very long time we were afraid of what the next move of those extremely powerful aliens might be, and we kept asking our scientists about the best way to try something against their superior weapon, with no effect in the end." The colonel paused for a while, then he decidedly stated. "But now we have the answer. We know what they want from us."

"That being…?" the aged man asked, incapable of really believing that he was going to be given an explanation to it all, after so many years of doubts and worries. *What was going to happen now?*

"We have just learned of a sort of new, imminent war that is going to start soon between two different factions, and we have been asked to side with one of them: with the Hulowrs. The aliens themselves have asked us for our consent to be part of their coalition."

"What? Being in a coalition along with them? How come? And why did they make us such an offer after everything that happened before?" Robert simply refused to believe such a statement.

"They need allies. Apparently that new war of theirs needs many more soldiers than they have now, and they have asked us to be the supporting party in their struggle that has already started in this part of space…" the colonel said.

"Would they allow us to be equal to them?"

"Yes, I see what you are suggesting…" Voewt smirked "Indeed, they don't seem to be planning to use our army as cannon fodder, as they have also promised to remove—once and for all—the fear of their weapon out of the mind of our military troops. This is a sign of benevolence towards us, so they say, and also the best way to show us that they don't want to consider our troops as lesser allies, people that they can easily get rid of once their present battles are over."

"What if they don't keep their promise in the end, sir?" Robert asked the other.

"What other options do we have? Of course, we could refuse their offer, given the previous circumstances, but what would happen next? Wouldn't they simply come here and use our home planet and all of our colonies as military bases, once they had wiped humans out completely? Of course they could, and in such a case we would have nothing left, no other way to keep our civilization alive. And there would be nothing left to negotiate with…On the other hand, if we accept what they appear to be giving us, we can enter this coalition they are proposing and maybe even come out ahead at the end of the war: think of alien technology, new arms and equipment, and new trade agreements in the end."

"But they haven't exactly put the matter under such terms so far, sir," said the professor.

"True, indeed. On the other hand, they also haven't told us: 'be in our coalition as allies or be destroyed'. Which means something, according to our government, anyway…" the colonel said.

"You have a point, sir, for sure. But what do you know about the present enemies of the Hulowrs?"

"Nothing at all. Our probes have detected a few movements of unfamiliar alien ships in deep outer space, but there's been no message from them, nor have they attacked, so far." A short silence followed the officer's words.

"What if we side with the enemies of the Hulowrs? After all, aren't the Hulowrs the adversaries who stopped our space race down on Auxesia, the aliens who defeated us all?"

"Well, that is not how our politicians think nowadays. Of course, if we decided not to side with them, we might stay out of that oncoming confrontation, but what good would come for mankind by bowing out of the fight? We would get nothing in the end, or we might even end up being in the middle of an interplanetary war that involves two powerful armies, with the chance to become the operational area of one of the two sides, and without our consent. And I can't even imagine how we can think about resisting such overwhelming adversaries as the ones who so easily defeated us before—or their present opponents— all alone, without any clear support from the Hulowrs." Voewt eyed him for a moment.

"So, we are caught in the middle, and we have to choose to side with one of the two." Robert considered.

"The decision has been already made, and it's the obvious one. There are some details I can't discuss with you now, given the secrecy involved in it all, but soon a statement will come down from General Headquarters. I just wanted you to know about the recent development of the Humans-Hulowrs relationship, given all that you and your recon team went through years ago."

"There are only two of us left nowadays, as far as I know: me and Hoet Franks, the one who was appointed to connect to our communication system on that world. All the others are dead.

"You're wrong." The Colonel disagreed with him. "It's true that the many men and women involved in that operation have already passed away so far, a lot of them died because of their old age or during the subsequent three small wars against the Thrt. But out of a personnel deployment of one hundred and fifty-five thousand military troops at that time, you are the last one that is still alive today. Officer Hoet Franks died two years ago in one of our medical facilities. He never completely recovered from that terrible experience, the same as you know that happened to many other soldiers dropped to Auxesia. We've kept his passing a secret so far. So, it's only you, you are truly the last surviving soldier of that unlucky expeditionary force."

"I see. So, are they going to remove that damn curse from my brain that forcibly put me out of full operational service long ago and made me turn to teaching instead of fighting and having a brilliant military career?" Robert asked the colonel before him.

"Actually, that is the point. They will allow the minds of all humans—be they civilian or military—to be protected for the future against the effects of the use of the flaming bomb weapon, but they expressly requested that the ones who were affected at that time be maintained exactly as they were…That means you, only you. This is to be used as a means of intimidation for future generation, a clear reminder of what might happen again if we only try to betray the Hulowrs one day." Voewt revealed.

"What…? Are you implying that…are you saying…?" were the spluttering words Robert uttered at that moment.

"Of course, as you can imagine we accepted! What else could we do?" the colonel stated in a plain tone.

"So…why…? What?" Robert began, without a better or stronger command of his language.

"We're very sorry for you being left in such a condition. Anyway, it will not last for long…"

Robert raised his eyes, then he understood. "Do you mean that…"

"Exactly, over the course of the war following our entry into the new coalition, the Hulowrs will have to come to the surroundings of our External Boundary, and they will also have to settle some outpost nearby, probably even on Earth itself. So they will be near the place where you are now, and given the effects their weapon is still supposed to have on humans, you'll sense the recurring pain of the past use of it."

"But this is…how can you do this to me?"

"There is no other way. The aliens were very clear about it. I'm so sorry about what will happen to you in the near future. Anyway, it will not last for long…you're old now and your life expectancy isn't very long, you know. What you'll undergo is in the interest of mankind. The Hulowrs demanded this as a clear warning for us all, for you to be kept alive so that it's possible for the pain and suffering to be shown publicly—in order to remind all of us of what might be. I'm so sorry for you, again, but this is in the interest of mankind." That being said, he activated a button that soon brought the two officers waiting outside the door return and direct the upset and very reluctant Captain outside.

"What other choice did we have?" the Colonel said as he watched the old man being forcibly taken out of the room. "*I only hope you do not have to suffer for too long…Your sacrifice will not be forgotten…*

Rituals

By Rick Partlow

McKay was pushed into his acceleration couch as the lander rocketed away from her monolithic mothership, leaping with a lemming's enthusiasm toward the sullen planet below.

It's just another balls-in, he repeated silently, just another simulation. That was what he'd told himself on every Ballistic Insertion he'd experienced since he'd enlisted. It had worked, too, back when he'd been a private, green and fresh out of college. But now he was Second Lieutenant Jason McKay, commanding his own reaction squad, and that blue-green hemisphere that filled the forward viewscreens wasn't Earth. He was some twenty light-years from home, above the second world out from 82 Eridani, and it was all too real.

Whatever could have possessed me, he wondered, *to go to Officer's Candidate School?*

"Sir?" Sergeant Wolczk turned to him, confusion furling his Cro-Magnonesque brows. McKay realized with a start that he must have unconsciously vocalized part of that internal question.

"Uh...I was just asking if everything was secure, Gunny," McKay lied.

"Oh, yes, sir," the burly Marine sergeant said with a grin. "All the troops're strapped in, and everything's battened down."

"Good. You okay back there, Constable Mei?" McKay craned his neck around to speak to the man behind him. Looking lost in the smallest combat armor they'd been able to find, Mei-Shin Lao made an unlikely cop; but the spindly, fiftyish Laotian was the chief constable of Inferno, one of the roughest colony worlds of the Republic.

"Yes, I am quite secure, thank you," Mei replied.

"When the guano hits the turbines, stick close to me," McKay told him. "Don't get me wrong," he hastened to add, "I'm sure you can handle yourself, but Marines train to a certain attack pattern, and if you're not in a 'friendly' zone, they're likely to pump you first and ID the remains later."

"I will do as you suggest, Lieutenant. Thank you for your concern."

"It'd be a good idea for you to watch where you're moving too, Captain," McKay told the other occupant of the command compartment who sat beside, and dwarfed by comparison, Constable Mei. Captain Miguel Hernandez was a fair-haired titan in the bulky, black armor of the Colonial Guard, a weighty rocket rifle wedged between his knees.

"I will go where I damn well please, McKay!" the Argentinian snapped. "And I still plan to file an official protest with the governor about this unacceptable command structure. I am your superior officer, and I should be leading this attack."

"Regulations, Captain," McKay reminded him, visibly unimpressed with the man. "Only a Marine officer can lead Marines in a combat situation."

"Then it should be Guard troops leading the assault!" The big man smacked the plastic lining on the bulkhead with his armor-gloved fist.

"Nearest Guard troops are two days out, on Eden," McKay said, a flush of heat traveling swiftly up the back of his neck. "It's only blind luck we were this close to Inferno. I assume you'd like to retake the base while some of your soldiers are still alive?"

The Captain's eyes narrowed in a look meant to seem threatening but rendered ludicrous by the convergence of the man's bushy blond eyebrows. "I find your tone offensive, Lieutenant."

"That's a damn shame," McKay grunted, feeling the checks slip off his temper. He was millimeters from a court-martial offense when the lander's deorbit burn ended and free-fall rescued him. "If you'll excuse me, I'm going to brief my squad."

Unstrapping himself, McKay grabbed a handhold and shoved himself through the hatchway back into the troop compartment. Sergeant Wolczk scrambled to follow, moving in the null gravity with practiced ease.

"Ten-shut!" Wolczk's voice cut through the squad's chatter as the pair halted themselves inside the compartment.

The squad fell silent and turned in their acceleration couches to face McKay. He silently scanned the faces of the nine men and three women. Remembering their names wasn't too difficult: they were emblazoned on the breasts of their fatigues. What was hard was attaching anything meaningful to those names. Out of the twelve, he could only put together as much as a thumbnail sketch of three.

Closest to him was Corporal Ari Shamir, the quiet young Israeli who always seemed to be reading something. Next to the corporal was Shawn Dobbs, a giant of a man who McKay knew didn't give a damn for officers in general and him in particular. Over in the corner was Joanna Corson, the skinny, Canadian private with the squeaky voice that everyone was always mimicking. He'd only been in command for four months, and almost half of that had been spent unconscious in the g-tanks. He wished he knew them better...but it was probably better that he didn't.

"It's about a half-hour till we hit atmosphere," McKay announced in what he hoped was a calm, steady voice. "You know the score. Some local politician name'a Luan Shou Shin has the Asian immigrants in New Saigon stirred up about the local conditions. He's got about a hundred of them together—mostly Pan Asian Alliance exiles from the Uprising—and they took Inferno's Colonial Guard armory, got ahold of some heavy weapons. The local cops only have antipersonnel, riot-control stuff, so they called on us to pull the CeeGee's ass out of the fire."

"So what else is new?" somebody muttered.

"What kinds of heavy weapons are we talking about, sir?" Shamir asked.

"Rocket rifles, assault cannons, lots of heavy personal armor," McKay replied. "Maybe a couple of attack vehicles. Luan and his people have combat experience, but we don't know if they're familiar with high-tech targeting systems. Standard tactics, though: hit 'em hard and fast, and hit 'em again before they know what's happening. Take out their vehicles first, then penetrate the building. I wish we could just level the place, but we've got to bust out the Guard troops they're holding."

"How'd they take the armory in the first place?" asked a skinny private with ears two sizes too big for his head. His name was...Nichols, that was it.

"Inside help: civilians working maintenance. They suckered everyone in, gassed them with their own security system. The good captain managed to escape to warn the cops and they called us...we were the closest thing available since the *Bradley* was refueling at the solar antimatter factory. Mei and Hernandez managed to get to the planet's only shuttle and came up to help us coordinate the attack."

"Damn CeeGee's were always a bunch of amateurs," Dobbs muttered.

"At ease with that crap, Dobbs!" Wolczk snapped.

"Just stay tight and listen to Gunny and we'll all get through this," McKay finished, hoping he sounded convincing to them...because he sure as hell didn't believe it himself.

Wind buffeted the bulbous lander as it descended through the upper layers of Inferno's atmosphere, the ship's delta wings grabbing furtively at the gradually thickening air, its heat shielding glowing with ionized fire. This was the part of a balls-in that always made McKay sweat: the moment between the shutdown of the hydrogen-fluorine rockets and the start-up of the ramjets.

The jets won't start! his mind screamed at him. *We're all going to die!*

But the crew in the cockpit was expert; the jets sucked in air and ignited, kicking them all soundly in the pants. McKay resumed breathing and hit the intercom switch on the bulkhead beside him.

"All right, boys and girls," he announced, "we de-ass in twelve minutes. Wait for the smoke and use your thermal sights. Everyone secure helmets and check your seals. Good luck and good hunting."

"Good hunting?" Mei repeated, cocking an eyebrow.

"Just a kind of ritual." McKay shrugged uncomfortably, not wanting to go into how he had picked up the expression from a previous commander. He slipped on his armored battle helmet and secured its airtight yoke.

"Oh, yes." Mei laughed humorlessly. "A ritual." He pulled on his borrowed helm and continued the conversation through its comlink. "All cultures have their rituals, do they not, Lieutenant?"

"I guess," McKay muttered, wishing the man would drop it.

"And what we are about to do," Mei continued, caressing the assault rifle strapped across his chest, "is surely the oldest ritual of all."

New Saigon was a city in flames. It hardly seemed possible in an age of plastiform buildings, electric-powered transportation, fusion generators, and beamed energy transmission, but Inferno was not Earth. Many buildings were constructed out of native wood, and many vehicles ran on methane or alcohol. Add to that mixture several dozen self-styled revolutionaries liberally tossing around firebombs the night before, stir vigorously, and *voila!* one family-sized bonfire.

People had stampeded through the packed-dirt streets of the low, sprawling town, screaming in uncontrolled panic, leaving their possessions behind, abandoning the city to its fate and heading down the river as the flames burned high into the early hours of the morning. But that had been last night. Now the fires burned in solitude, those not lucky enough to escape the flames left as smoldering corpses in the smoking wreckage.

The living remnants of the city were gathered into two armed camps. The Exiles under Luan Shou-Shin were holed up inside the Colonial Guard planetary armory, the largest building in New Saigon. Attack vehicles prowled the street without, waiting for the assault they expected from the constabulary unit out of

Peiping, the nearest city, whom they assumed Mei's people had called. Mei's constables, meanwhile, were barricaded in the local Government Center, waiting for something more potent than a handful of riot police.

And on the river that bordered the city on the east, some of the more daring souls watched from the shelter of crudely-built wooden rafts to see if or when the two groups would finally decide to shoot it out. For hours, they had been disappointed: nothing had happened.

Until an ear-splitting sonic boom shattered every window left intact in the city.

The light-gray Fleet Marine lander bled off speed as it curved back around the rain-sodden fields west of the city, then came in low and slow two streets behind the armory, belching thick clouds of dark, electrostatically-charged smoke that obscured eye and electronic sensor alike. It hovered for a scant moment less than two meters above the street, vectored thrust jets swirling the smoke around it as a rear egress hatch flew open and sixteen figures dropped into the darkness below. Its job done, the lander moved on to circle the armory, still trailing smoke, and headed west to the farmlands to touch down lightly on its VTOL jets.

Buried in gouts of impenetrable fog, the two attack vehicles on the street fired blindly and desperately, filling the air with missiles, explosive shells and laser pulses, until first one then the other exploded in an incandescent cloud of molten metal, as missiles tipped with chemical hyperexplosives found their weak spots. The two Marines responsible dropped their shoulder-fired launchers, unslung their autorifles, and ran to join the rest of the squad.

"Shamir," Gunny Wolczk radioed, "take your group and hit the rear entrance. The rest of you follow the lieutenant and me."

Before he had finished speaking, a half-dozen Pan Asians in CeeGee armor scrambled out of the front entrance firing rocket rifles at targets whose positions they only half-understood from their helmets' unfamiliar optics.

Dobbs and LeClerc swung around their gimbal-mounted, dual-drum-fed autoguns, received the signal tones from their helmet-gun targeting links, and opened up on the revolutionaries. Their nearly-recoilless, polymer autoguns spat out a deadly barrage of alternating tungsten penetrators and hyperexplosive 12mm frag rounds, the one-two punch hammering through the thick armor and butchering the men within, turning the six defenders into scrap metal and scattered body parts in less than a second.

"Smoke, Peterson," Wolczk ordered. The private pulled a pair of canisters out of a belt pouch, jerked out their pins and tossed them through the big, open double doors, filling the entrance corridor with clouds of inky smoke that spread through the building as quickly as the fire had spread through the city.

With the entrance cleared, Dobbs ducked inside first, followed by Wolczk, while McKay and his two guests led the remainder of the group in, leaving LeClerc to guard the rear. Confused, unarmored Exiles, running helter-skelter through the hallways, balked at the sight of the invading Marines and tried to bring up appropriated weapons—or tried to turn and run the other way—but were either blown into hamburger by Dobb's gun or pumped with tantalum-core 6mm slugs from the others' rifles.

"Command station to the left," Hernandez announced, running up beside McKay, his armored boots ringing on the floor like hammer blows.

"Captain," McKay instructed, "go with Peterson and LeClerc and secure the command station. If you can, try to grab someone alive and find out if all of your people are being held in the detention cells downstairs. That's where we'll be headed. Call me if you find anything."

"As you say," the Guard officer agreed, noticeably more cooperative now that the adrenaline had begun to pump. "But I cannot promise I will be able to restrain myself with any of these vermin."

He headed off to the left, followed by the two Marines.

"He's a wonderful guy," Wolczk muttered to McKay over their private channel.

"Yeah. C'mon, Gunny, let's go find those thumb-fingered CeeGee's." He switched over to Mei's channel. "You doing okay, Constable?"

"Fine, thank you," Mei said calmly, even as he spun on his heel and put a single round into an incoming rifleman.

McKay grinned. "I can see that you are. All right, Dobbs, take point. Casey, watch our backs."

The six men set off at a brisk trot, disdaining the nearby elevator banks for the emergency stairwell while PFC Casey covered their backs with another smoke grenade. The door to the stairwell was locked...and shortly it was nonexistent, after Dobbs let it have a top-to-bottom burst. He led the way and the others filed through behind him.

Glancing at Dobbs, McKay idly entertained the thought that the man must be wearing an industrial exoskeleton under his armor. Even with what had to be forty-five kilos of gun, armor, and ammo, the big man took the stairs three at a time.

They reached the door to the detention level unopposed, Wolczk trying it and finding it locked. Dobbs was about to do his number on it when McKay got a transmission over his helmet commlink and put a restraining hand on the gunner's arm.

"Wait a second," McKay ordered. "What was that?"

"This is Captain Hernandez," the Argentinean repeated. "I have the command station secured, but your trooper Peterson is dead."

"Damn!" McKay hissed, feeling like he'd been kicked in the nuts. "Did...did you capture anyone alive?"

"Not yet. But the security scanners are working—I have the detention level on the screen. It appears that all of my men are being held there, and they are heavily guarded: a dozen men, five in armor, one with an assault cannon."

"What's the layout?"

"The ones in armor are patrolling the halls; the one with the heavy gun is on your right. The seven others are in the detention control center at the left end, about fifty meters down the hall."

"Can you gas the ones in the control center?" McKay asked hopefully.

"Negative. The gas cells are dry. If you will wait, we will come down to aid you..."

"No," McKay cut him off. "I need you to coordinate with Corporal Shamir. Get a hold of him and let him know if there's any concentrations of enemy and where they are. Try to find Mei's people..."

"I can see them on the outside scanners already," Hernandez interrupted. "They're approaching the front entrance—about twenty of them."

"All right," McKay sighed. "Contact Corporal Shamir and get them working together. We're going to free your men. I'll call you when the smoke clears. McKay out."

He turned back to his half-squad. "All right, let's do it by the numbers. The second Dobbs takes out that door, I want Casey to toss in a smoke grenade. We got a gunner on the right, four others in armor up and down the hall, plus seven regulars at the end of the corridor. Nichols, you draw the gunner's fire, give Dobbs enough time to get in and nail him. Gunny, you and me'll try to take out the guys on the left quick with grenades. Watch your aim though—we got CeeGees on both sides of the hall.

"Casey, you and Mei wait until the hall is clear, then go take the detention control center. Use gas grenades, if possible, but don't take any chances. Everybody ready?"

A chorus of "Aye, sir" answered him as Casey pulled out his last smoke grenade. McKay fed a rocket-assisted antiarmor grenade into the launcher mated to the side of his autorifle, and the others followed his example. "Okay, Dobbs, do it!"

Dobbs squeezed the trigger of his weapon, lifting the muzzle from the base of the door upwards, blowing it into scattered bits of debris with a metallic roar. Casey chucked in his smoke bomb, then Nichols followed it through the doorway, rolling into a crouch in the center of a corridor lined with transparent plastiform cell doors. Clouds of smoke billowing around him, Nichols fired his grenade launcher by reflex at the first target he saw, an armored guard standing just to the right and in front of the assault gunner. The antiarmor grenade took the man at belt level and blew him in half in a deafening explosion that splattered everything within ten meters with blood and metal fragments.

The Pan Asian gunner was momentarily startled, but he was also a combat veteran. He swung around his twenty-kilo weapon and fired two rounds at Nichols through the smoke. Even as the gunner was firing, Dobbs was squeezing through the stairwell door behind Nichols and more armored troops were running up from the left, taking wild shots at the incoming Marines.

The gunner's volley missed Nichols by a good meter, the rocket-assisted rounds impacting a cell door with a double-thunderclap, punctuated by the screams of the Guard soldiers within. Dobbs growled deep in his throat and hosed the gunner with a ten-round burst of 12mm that chewed up the firing mechanism of the rebel's cannon before decapitating him.

Behind Dobbs, Wolczk and McKay intercepted the advancing armored troops with a pair of rocket grenades, each of them downing a man with explosions that shook the halls. That left one armored revolutionary, and no time for the two Marines to reload their launchers, Constable Mei not yet through the doorway, and Dobbs facing the other direction.

"Dobbs!" was all McKay had time to say as he and Wolczk and the Asian revolutionary opened up with their rifles almost simultaneously.

McKay could see his shots ricocheting off the heavy armor on the man's chest and tried to adjust upward toward the faceplate, but a stream of smoke-trails was already erupting from the Exile's rocket rifle. All McKay could do was stare in helpless amazement as two of the 15mm, gyrostabilized minirockets punched through the honeycomb boron-ceramic armor over Wolczk's chest and blew a fist-sized hole in his back.

An eyeblink later, the gunner was dismembered by a long burst from Dobb's autogun, but Jason's horrified gaze was glued to the Gunny. His body seemed to float to the floor with impossible slowness, and through his faceplate Jason could see a look not of pain or fear but of profound confusion. Those squinting, half-alive eyes locked with McKay's, and for one, uncanny moment he felt frozen in time, as if Gunny Wolczk's death were such an unnatural thing that the universe wouldn't allow it to occur. But then his shoulders touched the floor, breaking the spell, and Casey and Mei took off at a double-time down the corridor toward the control center, leaving McKay and Dobbs gaping in disbelief at the lifeless body of Gunnery

Sergeant Van Wolczk. McKay heard someone moaning softly, like a man slowly dying, and realized that it was coming from him.

Nichols, his brain whispered like some stranger clearing his throat for attention. *Where's Nichols?*

As if in response to his thoughts, an eddy of smoke rose from the floor to reveal Private Arturo Nichols sprawled face-down a few meters away.

"Aw Jesus." McKay knelt beside him and gently turned the eighteen-year-old over, but he was gone, his throat blown out by a minirocket. "Dobbs!" McKay ordered through clenched teeth. "Go help Casey—now!"

"Yes...aye, sir." The big man nodded slowly, tearing his gaze away from the sergeant and turning to run down the corridor as gunshots sounded from the direction of the detention control center.

McKay left the two bodies and walked over to the cell door that had been shattered by the assault cannon. There were seven men inside of it, all dressed in the light-green duty fatigues of the Colonial Guard. Three of them were clearly dead, their uniforms shredded from the fragments both of the door and the Asian revolutionary's cannon rounds. The other four were alive, but they had seen better days.

One was conscious: a slim, young East African with a broken and swollen nose and blood running from his left ear. He looked up at McKay, blinking his eyes to clear them, and tried to get to his knees, coughing from the smoke drifting down the corridor.

"Who are you?" he asked in accented English.

"Marines," McKay told him over his helmet's external speaker. Offering a hand, he pulled the soldier to his feet. "Are you okay?"

He shook his head. "I can't hear you so good, but I want to fight them."

"Come on then," McKay urged, waving for the man to follow. The soldier grabbed a rocket rifle from one of the dead rebels and hefted the heavy weapon confidently.

McKay glanced around him. There were dozens of other Guard troops in the other cells in the corridor, pounding soundlessly, screaming without being heard behind the soundproof doors. Without a computer key card, McKay realized, there was no way to open the cells except from the control center. Jason signaled for them to wait with an upheld hand, and they seemed to relax.

"Casey, this is McKay," he radioed. "Sitrep."

"Control center is ours, sir," Casey reported. "We've got a couple live ones. They say Luan Shou Shin's somewhere on this level."

"Right. Stay there till you hear from Shamir. See if you can get the cell doors unlocked."

"We'll try, sir. It may take a while...some of the control boards were hit."

"Do your best."

"Sir," Casey wondered, "what about Luan?"

"Don't worry," McKay replied grimly. "I'm going to find him. McKay out." The Lieutenant turned to his new-found ally, who appeared to be getting impatient. "C'mon," he motioned. "We've got to find..." He was interrupted by the ringing echo of a gunshot, and a shrill scream somewhere off to his right. "Dammit!"

Jason took off headlong down the corridor with the African at his heels. Rounding a curve to the left, they saw a tall, rakishly-mustached Chinese male whom Jason recognized from the threat briefings as Luan Shou Shin calmly firing a pistol into an open cell of restrainer-bound Colonial Guard troops. Two were already dead, and he was lining up on a third...

"Son of a bitch!" Jason opened up with his autorifle, the deep-throated stutter of his weapon in sharp contrast with the muted cough of the young Guardsman's rocket rifle.

The Exile leader danced backwards under the impact of half a magazine of McKay's 6mm slugs before a pair of minirockets blew his skull apart like a water balloon. The African soldier, his eyes wide and wild, kept pumping round after round into the corpse until his weapon went dry. What was left of Luan by the time the rifle's ammo drum hit empty bore little resemblance to a human being.

By instinct more than anything else, McKay swept the area with his helmet sensors, but saw only more imprisoned Guard troops. Letting out a deep sigh, Jason felt a shudder run through him, all the fear and anger and hatred welling up inside his gut, rising like a gorge in his throat.

It shouldn't have happened like this. They had done everything by the book—no mistakes—but Gunny and the rest were still dead. McKay had to shake his head to dispel the memory of the experienced gunnery sergeant greeting his new lieutenant, merged with the lingering image of the same man's limp and lifeless body. Eventually, he realized that someone was speaking to him over his helmet commlink.

"...tenant McKay, are you there, sir?" It was Shamir.

"I'm here. Report." He was surprised at how calm his voice was.

"The base is clean, sir." Shamir's voice told of physical and emotional exhaustion. "No resistance left anywhere if Captain Hernandez is reading the sensors correctly." A long pause, and McKay could hear him taking a deep breath. "We lost Corson and Dundee. Richards and Mitchell are wounded, but they should both pull through."

"Call the lander," McKay ordered, fighting to keep his brain working just a little longer. "Have them contact the *Bradley*, send out a medical unit. Get Mei's people to set up a temporary hospital till we can evac the wounded. Get some stretchers down to the detention level—some of the CeeGees'll need treatment."

"Aye, sir."

"Oh, and Shamir..." McKay trailed off, his voice catching in his throat. "You're acting sergeant."

"Uh...yes, sir. I'm sorry, sir."

Jason leaned heavily against the wall and slid slowly down to the floor. He knew he should help the young African untie the CeeGees. He knew he should gather up his men and get them to the command center...but not just now.

It was about a half an hour later before McKay, Casey, and Dobbs made their way back up to the command center, leaving Mei and his cops on the detention level to care for the wounded. Small fires burned in places and the corridors were filled with drifting smoke that coated the walls with soot. Bodies of rebels—and a few of local police—littered the hallways, but McKay studiously avoided looking at them.

As the three Marines approached the entrance to the command center, they heard the sounds of some kind of disturbance from their destination: shouts, crashing furniture, and the unmistakable sound of flesh striking flesh. McKay was too drained to hurry—he just continued walking at a normal gait toward the wide open doorway.

"Tell me!" Hernandez's voice reached them before they came to the entrance. "Tell me where he is!" The smack of a fist into flesh echoed off the walls.

McKay came to the doorway and saw the brawny guard captain, *sans* armor, clutching a bound Vietnamese teenager by the shirtfront with one hand and slapping him with the other. Blood was already flowing from the youth's nose and mouth, and he looked only half-conscious.

"Captain Hernandez." McKay pulled off his helmet and tossed it and his rifle to Casey. "Just what are you doing with that Marine prisoner?" His voice was soft, but deadly as a loaded gun.

"McKay, you..." Hernandez spun around, but hesitated in mid-bluster. The grim set of McKay's jaw was enough to give even the arrogant Guard Captain pause. "I was attempting to force the whereabouts of Luan Shou Shin from this Exile scum we captured."

"Put him down," McKay ordered.

"I will have the truth from him," Hernandez insisted, voice rising like a child denied a toy. "This piece of shit is responsible for my personal humiliation! Having to run from the city like a child..."

"I said," McKay repeated, stepping up and punching the captain full in the face with a straight left, "put him down!"

Hernandez pitched over backward, hands going to his nose, while his prisoner slumped to his knees. The Guard Captain spat out a red blob, swearing through clenched teeth as he struggled to his feet.

"Bastard!" Hernandez started into a lunge for McKay, but Corporal Shamir appeared like a wraith, interposing his autorifle between the two officers.

"Don't," was all the Israeli said.

"Luan Shou Shin is dead," McKay told Hernandez, his voice more tired than angry. "I killed him, with the help of one of your men. Remember your men, Captain? The reason we didn't just bomb this building to rubble? The reason I just got five good people killed? I'll tell you one thing, Hernandez, it sure as hell wasn't to save your reputation. Why don't you go and see to your men, Captain? Why don't you just get the hell out of my sight."

Hernandez looked as if he were about to say something but reconsidered after a glance at Shamir's assault rifle. Wiping a hand across his chin, the captain turned on his heel and stomped out of the room.

McKay stepped over to the other side of the command center, where the two wounded Marines lay. Richards, a hard-muscled woman with hair shorter than McKay's and skin the color of dark chocolate leaned against the wall with half-closed eyes, her left thigh swathed in a thick field bandage. Mitchell, a wiry, pale teenager who'd joined their squad at the same time as McKay, was stretched out unconscious, an oxygen mask over his face and a soaked-through dressing taped to his right side. Jean LeClerc, bereft of both his helmet and his autogun, was leaning over Mitchell, checking his vital signs with a small, electronic sensor.

"How is he?" McKay asked the French Canadian.

LeClerc shrugged. "Lost a lot of blood. Got maybe three shattered ribs, a punctured right lung. He'll live, but he could use some attention, and soon." McKay nodded then went over to squat beside Richards.

"How're you doing, Private Richards?"

"Feeling no pain, sir," she said, grinning, eyes slightly out of focus. "Jean's got me pumped with some good shit."

"Her femur's broken," Jean told him, "but the artery's still intact. She'll be fine. They'll have it fused and she'll be walking in a few days."

"Good." Jason patted her on the shoulder. "You take it easy. The medtechs'll be here soon."

McKay straightened and moved to where Shamir was leaning on the commo board, talking to the lander. Jason sat on the edge of the panel and waited for the corporal to finish. The young Israeli finally signed off and looked over to his lieutenant.

"Lander says the medevac team'll be here in five minutes, sir."

"You did a good job taking this place," McKay told him honestly.

Shamir just nodded. His short, black hair was matted with sweat, and there were lines of exhaustion in his face. "Sir..." He trailed off helplessly.

"What?" McKay prompted.

"I don't understand why they did it, sir," he said, shaking his head. "They had to know they couldn't hold this place. Why didn't they just hit it and fade back into the crowd? Why wait here and get slaughtered?"

Jason started to answer but hesitated. In a moment like this, did the young corporal really want to hear his college professor's theories of terrorist tactics and symbolic martyrdom? Hell, what did that professor know about death?

"It's just a ritual, Ari," he sighed. "Just a ritual."

We hope that you enjoyed this title and look forward to many more to come. Please, leave us a review! Reviews matter to all of our authors.

Take a look at some of our other award-winning series at https://threeravenspublishing.com/series-universes/

Visit us at https://www.threeravenspublishing.com and sign up for our newsletter for the latest and greatest news on upcoming titles and events.

Other series and titles you might enjoy.

DECLAN FINN
DECLAN FINN
DECLAN FINN DECLAN FINN
Demons are Forever
Honor at STAKE
Live & Let Bite
Good to the Last Drop
The Dragon Award Nominated Series
FREE on Kindle Unlimited!

AVAILABLE ON
AMAZON
JOINT TASK FORCE
13
HOLDING THE LINE
BETWEEN HEAVEN AND HELL
13

MYSTERY,
MAGIC &
MAYHEM
WITH A TWIST
OF ROMANCE
J.F. POSTHUMUS
ON AMAZON
FIND ME
B.E.N.T.
BIOLOGIC   ENHANCED   NASCENT   TALENT

The Raven
and
The Crow
Michael K. Falciani
FIND ME
ON AMAZON

STARFLIGHT

IT CAME FROM THE
TRAILER PARK

3R
Three Ravens Publishing
Are you looking for fun, new fiction?
The FEATHER and the LAMP
CROSSWAYS
THE WAYMAN CHRONICLES
MICHAEL J ALLEN
LEGENDS
DARK STORM RISING
STAFF of CHAOS
The Written Word Will Never Be The Same…
https://www.threeravenspublishing.com
Veteran Owned and Operated

You can also keep up to date with our latest release announcements on Scifi.radio and get some of the best fandom programing on the planet.

Scifi for your Wifi

And don't forget to check out our other Sponsors and Affiliates

A southern Appalachian jewel for craft beer lovers, Buck Bald Brewing offers something for everyone. With delicious, locally brewed beverages from across the spectrum, Buck Bald Brewing offers craft brews that are consistently amazing.

From the dark and smooth Shesquatch Scottish ale, to the intense hops of Hippibilly IPA, to the puckering sour of the blackberry and cinnamon in Berry My Heart at the Trailer Park, and more than 60+ rotating brews, you'll find what you're looking for and more.

With smiling faces behind the bar ready to help you find your next favorite brew, a constantly rotating selection of delicious craft beverages, toe-tapping tunes always playing, and the biggest games on TV, you can kick your feet up in either Copperhill, Tennessee or Murphy, North Carolina and immerse yourself in the Buck Bald Brewing experience. So, come out, fill a pint, fill a growler, and fill your mind at your new favorite family-owned craft brewery.

To discover more visit us at buckbaldbrewing.com or follow us on Facebook @buckbaldbrewing and @buckbaldbrewingmurphy.

Vesper Wren's
TRAILER PARK
PIXIE
PUNCH
· A PEACH STRAWBERRY SELTZER ·
BUCK BALD BREWING

And don't forget to check out the latest edition of *Car Wars*

http://www.sjgames.com/car-wars/

Or the other amazing titles from
Steve Jackson Games

http://www.sjgames.com

…or the latest in the Car Warriors: Autoduel Chronicle fiction series.
https://threeravenspublishing.com/car-warriors-autoduel-chronicles/